SHH...

SIAN B. CLAVEN

Chapter One

*H*eather stepped off of the elevator and onto the eleventh floor of her office building where several people were rushing around, going between cubicles with packs of paperwork in their arms. Some of the people were on loud phone calls and others were furiously typing on their keyboards. One woman, with curly black hair, was standing near the elevator nervously. She was clearly waiting for Heather because as Heather took strides towards her office she fell in step with her, talking in a slight stammer.

"I can explain..." Jeremy, Heather's sign language interpreter, had stepped off the elevator with her and signed as Maria, the nervous intern, spoke; Heather held her hand up to stop both of them.

She signed, "Maria, go back to your cubicle," and Jeremy told Maria what she had signed before he followed Heather into her office.

Heather sat at her table and waited. Kayla walked in a few moments later and placed the documents Maria had left with her in front of her boss. Heather flipped through the file, her eyes scanning the pages quickly. She knew this client well and she couldn't believe an inexperienced intern thought they could handle an account as big as this. If their boss Henry found out... Heather didn't want to think about the amount of shit that would rain upon her as the intern's manager.

She put her phone on speaker so that Jeremy could interpret for her and dialed the client's number. She waited for Jason to answer, her lips dry so she licked them gently. Jeremy stood by her side, as he always did, ready to do what he needed to do to help her win back this client. Jason answered without a hello. "Heather? This had better be you."

"It's Heather," Jeremy said as she signed in response to Jeremy's signing to her, "And firstly, I would like to apologize that some idiotic now fired intern thought they could even look at your file."

"You're going to have to do a lot better than apologize, Heather," Jason started to raise his voice, "because that damn bitch confused me with Mercury Objectives and told me exactly how you value them over me by giving me their discount rates. Is that how you treat my business after all these years?"

Heather didn't even pale at what was being said. "I know, Jason, and Mercury Objectives is not my client, and I am pissed to know the kind of discounts I could have gotten for you. All I'm asking is for a chance to give you something even better."

Jason remained silent and Heather quickly dived in to say, "What if I said that instead of a discount, I could give you a five year fixed premium if you stay with us? And a discount on any new accounts you bring to me with a two year fixed premium?" Heather watched Jeremy, waiting for Jason's response.

"Your boss is going to murder you for giving me a deal like that, Heather; are you even authorized to do that?"

"You don't have to worry about that, Jason," Heather signed and Jeremy translated, "I do, all you have to do is give me a yes or a no so I know whether or not I'm drafting new paperwork for you."

"Then it's a yes, and Heather, I want that new paperwork by the end of today or the deal's off."

The phone clicked and went dead, and Jeremy finished signing to Heather what Jason had said and explained the call was over. Heather sat back and sighed, rubbing her temples with her index fingers before pressing the intercom to summon Kayla. Once her receptionist had walked in, she signed again while Jeremy said, "Kayla, please tell Maria she's fired and put out an advertisement for a new intern. Let's get a guy this time; women are too power hungry and have something to prove. I can't deal with that drama. Also, I have a feeling Henry will want to see me now so hold all my calls."

"Yes ma'am," Kayla said before strolling out the door again.

Heather glanced at Jeremy who signed, "Henry is either going to thank you or fire you."

Heather shrugged and stood up, signing, "There's only one way to find out."

They both walked out of the office and back towards the elevator, only this time instead of feeling confident, Heather felt worried she'd just cost herself her job.

~

"You promised him what?" Henry seethed. He wanted to shout and perform, but he was actually at a loss for words. On a normal day, he might have even thrown a chair across the room.

"It's a huge account," Jeremy translated. "The company would lose more if Jason left than if we did a fixed premium."

"Heather, you seriously have some balls coming in here saying you made a promise like that." Henry took out a cigar and lit it. Most bosses did that to celebrate or look smart, Henry did it as a bad habit. He didn't even care about indoor no smoking policies. His building, his rules as he liked to say. He puffed out a large cloud of smoke and shook his head in disbelief before nodding. "Well, draw up the paperwork and get it to him; what are you still doing here?"

"Well, I wanted to ask about my promotion, sir," Jeremy said. "You said you'd let me know today if I got the position I applied for."

"Honey, you're too valuable where you are to put you in a higher position, especially with your limitations. I gave the job to Wade." Henry said it without looking at her and Heather felt the sting of betrayal in her chest. This promotion had been all she had been working towards for the last five years of her career. Never once had her *limitations*, her inability to hear or speak, ever come into question when it came to her doing her job. She wanted to bite back, to fight back, but Jeremy placed a hand on her shoulder and shook his head. She stood up and nodded, before striding out of the smoky room. Once in the elevator, Heather grunted her frustration and punched the wall of the small space before biting her lip in pain. Jeremy watched her sadly, signing, "I'm sorry. He's an asshole."

Heather shook her head and signed, "I don't want to talk about it."

They didn't speak to each other again until they reached the door of Heather's office, when she stopped and signed, "Can you go grab a coffee or something? I'd like to phone Andrew."

Jeremy nodded, giving her a moment to chat to her husband alone; he left without another word.

Heather was grateful for that; she didn't want to discuss her problems with Jeremy even though he was aware of them. She didn't want him to see how emotional she was really feeling. She shut her door and drew the blinds, sending an IM to Kayla not to disturb her before she sat at her computer and video called her husband. As soon as Andrew answered she burst into tears and it was a while before she was able to sign to him what had happened.

Once she had managed to explain the entire situation, she could see he was livid on her behalf. It wasn't just about the fact that she was skipped over for a promotion for being disabled, it was the fact that she was better than Wade despite being disabled. She was suited for the job, in every aspect, and being disabled did not hold her back. She wasn't crying out of sadness but out of frustration, and she knew her husband would understand. She worked so hard and had sacrificed so much time with her family, and it had amounted to nothing.

"I'm so sorry, babe," Andrew signed, "I know how badly you wanted the promotion and how hard you have worked for it. They don't deserve you at that shitty company."

"I just wish that I could find a company as big as this one and be appreciated for what I'm worth," she explained. "For fuck's sake, I am worth more than this. I hate that they use my disability as a reason to hold me back."

Andrew didn't say anything for a while, but Heather recognized the look on his face; the cogs were turning in that brain of his and he was clearly thinking of something. Nothing would fix this though; Henry had already given the promotion to Wade on grounds of her being disabled, so unless some miracle happened where she could suddenly hear and speak, there was no way she could compete with that decision.

"Don't worry, babe, when one door closes, another opens," Andrew signed. "I'll see you later. Love you."

"Love you," she signed before killing the call.

Jeremy walked back in with two cups of coffee and she smiled softly, signing her thanks to him before taking her cup. She then started to draft the documents for Jason before sending them to Henry for approval. It was a bittersweet moment for her. She had pulled off an amazing save for the company, but had nothing really to show for it other than keeping a big corporate account under her belt, that and a fired intern.

Once the paperwork was done, Heather did something she hadn't done in years. She sent an email to Henry stating that she was taking the remainder of the day off. She then shut her computer off, not bothering to wait for a response, and let Kayla know she was unavailable for the remainder of the day before she left, leaving Kayla and Jeremy staring after her. Several others also stared after her, but she knew that Henry wouldn't really do anything; he wanted her there, promotion or not, because she was good at her job. She was too pissed to stay though and wanted to spend some time alone. Hell, she might even send an email when she got home and put in a request for some of her leave. Her daughter was on holiday soon, maybe they could go away together to Disneyland or something and spend some time together as a family.

She needed time to think, that she did know, so she drove home and parked in the garage and only then, when the garage door had fully closed and she was enclosed in darkness, did she let the tears flow... She sobbed into her arms at first, but then the anger took over and she started to punch her steering wheel and everywhere else she could reach. If she could scream she would and the thought that she couldn't, that the accident had taken even that from her, made her more frustrated and angry and she sobbed harder.

Eventually she slid down in her chair and simply cried, curling up as best as she could, feeling sorry for herself for the first time in a long time. It wasn't until the garage door slid open again that she slowly started to sit up but too late; she knew her husband had seen her slouched and crying. He parked his own car and got out, going to open her door for her.

"I'm so sorry," he signed. "Henry is a dick."

"Everything sucks," she signed, feeling childish.

"It does," he signed back. "Do you want some wine and cake?" he offered.

She nodded glumly but gave him a small smile. This was why she had married him after all; it was these small things that he did, that he knew about her. He took her hand and led her into their home. Their daughter was still at school and wouldn't be home for a while, so they went to the kitchen. Heather sat at the island in the center of the kitchen while Andrew poured her a glass of dry red wine and got some cake out of the fridge. He had clearly known what a day she was having from the call earlier and had gotten it to be ready when she came home. The joys of having a work from home husband.

They sat together and ate their cake, drank their wine, and while they did that the tears started anew. Andrew let Heather get it all out. She signed about how angry and disappointed she was, how she hated James Leech, the man who had caused the accident that had led to the emergency surgery that Heather had needed, all the surgery that had cost her, her hearing and speech fifteen years ago.

She hated Henry for holding her disability against her when he knew she was the best. She hated the fact that she couldn't hear Andrew or their daughter Kyra's voices. Andrew let her get it all off her chest until eventually she just sat there, staring at the half eaten cake on her plate.

"Feeling better?" he asked, tilting her head up to look at him.

"A little," she signed, "Thank you."

"Good, now you're not going to take your leave because I have something special planned for all that leave you've accumulated, okay?"

Heather raised an eyebrow. "What have you planned?" she asked.

"None of your business," Andrew signed with a smile. "All will be revealed soon," he added.

Heather rolled her eyes; Andrew knew she hated surprises and was all about instant gratification, but she would let him think he could play it out. Somehow she would find out what he was up to. Maybe Kyra would know what he had planned; she would question their daughter later.

"She doesn't," Andrew signed with a cheeky smile, "I know what you're thinking and I knew you would ask Kyra, so I didn't tell her."

"Just tell me," Heather signed. "Come on, Andrew, I've had the worst day ever; just tell me what the big surprise is. I hate surprises."

"Control freak," Andrew teased, laughing happily.

Heather crossed her arms and pretended to sulk with him, turning her head away as he tried to feed her some cake before he sighed and signed, "Fine, but you are the ruiner of all surprises and you have to live with that for the rest of your life, okay?"

"Okay," Heather signed happily.

"At least close your eyes," Andrew signed, "I'll tap your shoulder when you can open them."

Heather rolled her eyes again and closed them, sitting with her arms crossed.

It was an eerie feeling; she hated sitting with her eyes closed and waiting for something to happen. She always anticipated that something was going to jump out at her or grab her suddenly, and when Andrew did finally tap her on the shoulder, she did give a slight jump in her seat.

She could see him chuckle softly and she pulled a tongue at him before looking down in front of her at the pamphlet he had set down. She picked it up and read it curiously. The more she read, the wider her eyes grew until finally the tears started all over again, this time from happiness.

Chapter Two

"I don't understand," Jeremy signed to her the next day during lunch while they sat opposite each other eating, "How is this possible?"

"It's experimental, so Andrew did say I mustn't get my hopes up because there is a possibility the surgery won't work and of course there's therapy afterward, but after seeing my x-rays and medical history the doctor confirmed he believes I have a seventy-five percent chance of getting my hearing and voice back, possibly fully," Heather explained, her fingers flying excitedly about.

Jeremy's mouth dropped open and he signed, "I don't think I've ever been so happy at the possibility that I'm going to be jobless before. Did Henry okay the time off?"

"Andrew already cleared it with him before he signed me up for everything!" Heather clenched her fists excitedly and if she were able to, she would have shrieked loudly.

Jeremy couldn't stop grinning and signed quickly, "We should celebrate before you go, one last night of being unable to hear and speak. We should go to the deaf club and dance it up before you no longer qualify to go there."

Heather sighed. "No longer qualify to go there, now won't that be something," she signed. Jeremy reached over the table to give her hand a soft squeeze and she gave him a gentle smile. She was about to sign something to him when her phone vibrated and she looked at it. She rolled her eyes and signed, "Henry wants to see me, right now."

Jeremy rolled his eyes as well and they quickly finished their lunch, taking their coffee to go. They walked back towards the tall building that housed their offices on one of the busiest streets in the city. There were really only tall, grey buildings around here with no parks in sight, and Heather had once commented that it was a sad view. She wished to see more plants and greenery and had the dream of one day retiring to a beautiful farm somewhere in the countryside where she could enjoy the fresh air. For now though, her focus was building an amazing career she could retire from. That involved making Henry a happy boss, but when she walked into his office he looked anything but happy.

"Took you long enough, do I pay you to work here or sit around at cafes talking shit all day?" Henry raised his voice.

Jeremy quickly started to translate to Heather and she immediately put her coffee down to reply, but Henry cut her off. "Never mind, I have an important account I want you to take over and the Manager Director is here now in the board room. Drop whatever you are doing, walk in there and impress the shit out of him, or find a new job."

Heather was surprised by Henry; he had never spoken to her like that, let alone threatened her job, and she quickly went to collect a portfolio from her office before heading to the main board room. She was so shocked by how Henry had behaved that she didn't realize until she was all the way into the room that it was full up with all her work friends and her husband Andrew. A huge banner spelling "SURPRISE" was hung up behind them. When she looked up she nearly jumped out of her skin as they raised their hands above their head and shook them to indicate they were clapping in sign.

Heather smiled brightly and signed to ask Andrew what was going on.

"You are approved for the trial surgery and they want you this weekend, so we quickly arranged a surprise goodbye party. Henry helped!"

Heather turned around to find her boss standing behind her, arms crossed and a cheeky smile on his face. She grinned and swatted at him, signing while Jeremy translated, "I wondered why you spoke to me like that; it wasn't like you at all."

"And I never would, Heather, we really value you here which is why we have extended your leave by two months, all paid, so you can have additional therapy. We believe in you and believe this therapy is going work, and we know when you come back you're going to go from strength to strength."

Heather swallowed the large lump that developed in her throat and fought back the tears that were beginning to form. Andrew quickly came forward and wrapped his arms around his wife and let her melt against him. Everyone raised their hands again in happiness and clapped in sign and when Heather raised her head and saw this, she burst into tears and buried her head in his chest, enjoying the happiness that was radiating inside of her. She knew this was going to be a successful surgery and was excited for the next step in her life.

Three Months Later...

Andrew turned in his seat on the airplane to look at his daughter sleeping across from him, enjoying the benefits of business class to the fullest by stretching out in the seat and napping as they flew down to Mexico to see her mother for the first time in months. They had chatted through email, but Heather had not wanted to video call because she wanted to surprise them with the progress she had made after therapy. It hadn't been easy being away from her, but Kyra, as any ten year old would be, was excited to see her mother again.

Andrew reached out and stroked a loose strand of blonde hair out of his daughter's face and her eyes fluttered open.

"Are we there yet?" she asked sleepily, stretching her arms up and over her head.

Andrew looked out of his window and smiled. "Almost I think, maybe another fifteen minutes."

As though on cue the Fasten Seatbelt light came on and the Captain's voice sounded over the speaker system, "Ladies and Gentlemen, this is your pilot speaking. We hope you've had a great flight with us here on Greater American Airways. We welcome you to Mexico International Airport. The temperature is eighty-three degrees and sunny today, and we hope you enjoy your stay in the city. Thanks for flying Greater American Airways, until next time."

The speaker sounded off and Andrew helped Kyra get her seat back into the sitting position and got her buckled in for landing as the air hostesses started to make their rounds, checking the passengers were prepared for landing and taking anything they could throw away on behalf of their charges. Andrew felt slightly nervous about seeing Heather again, wondering just how successful the surgery was and whether or not she was happy or disappointed. He didn't know what to expect, but he knew no matter what he loved Heather more than anything, and that he had loved her since they had met. Heather had never heard their daughter's voice, or his, and they had never heard her speak, so this was a big step for their little family and it was nerve-wracking.

He had prepared Kyra as best as he could, not wanting her to get her hopes up but at the same time wanting her to be excited for her mom in case there was even a small chance that her mom could hear even with the help of a hearing aid or implant. These thoughts had been reeling inside of Andrew's head for weeks and he had not had anyone to share them with. Both sets of parents had long ago passed away and they had no siblings, so it was just them, and he didn't want to share this kind of personal feeling with friends or co-workers. Well, he didn't really have co-workers because he worked from home. He didn't want to share this with Heather's co-workers because he knew she would flip out if they in any way questioned Heather.

The plane landed and Andrew collected their bags from the overhead compartment before, to Kyra's abject horror, he took his daughter's hand and led her off the plane. He did it without thinking about how uncool it looked and when he did realize, he let her hand go with a hearty laugh. Kyra pulled a face, let her blonde fringe fall in front of her face to hide her embarrassment, and stuck her headphones on so she could ignore him. He rolled his eyes but continued to smile as he kept an eye on her, steering her with a tap to the shoulder every now and then to get her attention.

Once they collected their larger luggage, Andrew made her take her headphones off so she didn't get lost and managed to get them a cab to the hotel they were staying at, which was near the facility. They checked in and freshened up before Andrew made sure Kyra was finally ready to see Heather.

During the cab ride there he turned to his daughter who was staring thoughtfully out the window. "Are you nervous?" he asked quietly.

"A little," she said, "I'm nervous that it didn't work and she's sad."

"I'm sure she would have let us know," he assured her.

Kyra nodded and in true pre-teen fashion, put her headphones on so she didn't have to talk about the subject anymore. Andrew smiled at his daughter and looked out his window, taking in the scenery while he could. They were only here overnight to get Heather and were flying home tomorrow. He had never been to Mexico before and this was a beautiful city, although if you looked close enough you could see past the tourist attractions and tell how poor the people really were. Andrew was used to that, having been to Africa on humanitarian missions in his youth. There was always more to a place than what first met the eyes.

The cab dropped them off outside a beautiful but ghostly looking building, and it seemed even more haunted when they went inside. It was dead quiet and seemed almost abandoned until an elevator dinged and a doctor dressed in a white lab coat walked out to meet them.

"Dr. Kent?" Andrew asked, extending his hand.

"Yes, yes, you must be Mr. Lawrence? And Miss Lawrence? Am I right?"

Andrew shook his hand. "That's right, please call me Andrew and this is Kyra."

Dr. Kent led them onto the elevator and pressed the button for the fifth floor. "Don't be surprised by the peace and quiet, we wanted somewhere peaceful for the patients to recover, and noise control was key."

Kyra had slipped her headphones off so she could hear what the doctor was saying and she looked up at Andrew nervously.

Andrew put a hand on her shoulder to reassure her and gave her a gentle squeeze. When the elevator opened up on the fifth floor there was more activity which set them both at ease. They could see other patients, nurses, and other doctors talking quietly and moving about on this floor.

"This way, please," Dr. Kent said as he walked ahead of them. They followed at a slightly faster walk as Dr. Kent was a tall, skinny man who took great but quiet strides. Andrew and Kyra were both nervous they would make too much noise with their footsteps and attract attention to themselves, and when one nurse burst out laughing, the sudden noise was so alarming they both jumped at the sound.

Dr. Kent chuckled, "It's not a hard and fast rule to be silent, noise is permitted, it's just preferred as new patients that are recovering can find loud noise to be painful. Ah, here we are. Heather Lawrence, room six five nine."

Dr. Kent stood at the door and knocked quietly. "Come in," a sensual voice called from inside, and both Kyra and Andrew's eyes widened.

Andrew looked at Dr. Kent quickly. "Was that..."

Dr. Kent simply smiled and Kyra rushed to open the door and get inside. "Mom?" she asked.

Heather was standing by the large window that overlooked the city, and she turned around as Kyra called her. She burst into tears at the sound of hearing Kyra called her 'mom' and she nodded. "Yes, baby," she said, and Kyra was reduced to tears as well. They both met in the middle of the room and hugged each other tightly, Kyra sobbing into Heather's bosom. "Your voice is so beautiful," she said.

Heather kissed her head and looked up at Andrew who realized his own tears were flowing freely. "Love..." he managed to choke out. "I love you," he said.

"I love you too..." Heather sobbed and before she could say anything else, Andrew closed the gap between them and kissed her deeply, wrapping his arms around both his daughter and wife and holding them tightly. Dr. Kent left as silently as he had led them there to enjoy their time together, happy that he had managed to bring one family back together.

It took a long while before they had stopped crying and they were able to look at each other without giggling or giving each other stupid smiles. Heather stroked Kyra's face softly and said, "I want to hear all about school and what you've been doing, and I don't ever want you to stop talking to me."

"I don't want you to stop talking to me; I won't ever listen through my headphones again," Kyra said, wiping her eyes on the back of her hand.

Andrew chuckled at this. "Now there's something. I've been trying to keep those things off her ears for the last three months and apparently all I had to do was give you a voice."

The small family all laughed together and continued to chitchat about how they loved each other until there was another knock at the door.

Dr. Kent had returned with a clipboard in hand and a nurse by his side.

"Mrs. Lawrence, we are so happy with your progress and that you've been reunited with your family, but before we can let you leave there is the matter of signing your exit paperwork and the nurse taking your vitals one last time."

"Of course," Heather croaked slightly and Andrew looked worried. She giggled and said, "It's because I'm emotional, don't worry."

Andrew smiled and nodded and stepped out of the way as the nurse came forward and started to examine Heather.

"Mr. Lawrence, you can come and complete the exit paperwork while the nurse is busy with your wife and then she can sign them on her way out," Dr. Kent said, leading Andrew and Kyra out to the lobby. Andrew picked up Heather's bags and took them with him as they left so they wouldn't have to come back for them. He filled in the paperwork and they waited for about fifteen minutes before Heather came out, ready to sign the paperwork to leave.

Kyra still hadn't put her headphones back on, not wanting to miss a word her mother said now that she could talk, and Andrew found this filled him with a sense of pride and love for his child and for his wife.

Chapter Three

From the moment they left the hospital until the moment they got home, the little family of three didn't stop talking. Mostly it was Andrew and Kyra asking Heather questions because they wanted her to talk and tell them stories, to tell them everything she had been through and more because they loved to listen to the sound of her voice. Kyra thought she would never tire of listening to her mother's voice, whether it was in love or anger, or any way at all. Andrew felt as though he was falling in love with Heather all over again and couldn't wait to be alone with her when they got home, but he knew they would have to wait.

Heather herself was exhausted but at the same time excited to be home. As the plane touched down she felt that although her body was tired, her soul was ready to take on the world and accomplish everything that had been denied to her before now. They caught a taxi from the airport and as they neared the house Andrew turned to his wife.

"Now, I want you to close your eyes tightly because I got something special for you," he explained.

"For me?" Heather asked with a grin.

"Especially for you, Mom," Kyra chimed in. "So no peeking."

"Okay," Heather said, shutting her eyes tightly.

The cab stopped outside of their house and Andrew guided Heather into their garage and told her to wait while he collected their luggage. After paying the driver and getting their luggage into the garage, he shut the door. "Okay, you can open your eyes."

Heather opened her eyes and looked around but only saw their vehicles parked in the garage like normal. "I don't get it…"

"The surprise is in the living room," Andrew explained. "But I had to give Kyra a head start to go set it up."

He offered her his hand and she smiled, lacing her fingers through his. He led her through the door and down the hallway through the dark house. Heather grinned and said, "I hope it's food, because I'm starving."

"It involves food so you're warm," Andrew said.

"Surprise!" Everyone shouted as they entered the room.

Heather jumped at the sudden eruption of noise before bursting out laughing. The room fell silent in surprise as they heard her laugh for the first time before they all started shrieking in excitement. It was friends from work, friends of Andrew's, friends they knew through friends of Kyra's, as well as neighbors. Heather cried happy tears as everyone surged forward to speak to her and hug her and welcome her back.

Andrew clapped his hands for attention and everyone turned to look at him. "Guys, guys, guys... if we can all calm down I'm sure we all want to hear Heather speak, so I'll let her stand on a chair and give one speech to everyone before we swamp her, okay?"

"Yeah, give a speech, Heather," someone shouted from the back, and soon everyone was chanting, "Speech! Speech! Speech!"

Heather grinned confidently as Andrew brought a chair for her to stand on and helped her onto it; she held her hands up and smiled.

"Thank you, everyone." She waited as everyone whooped at the sound of her voice, and once they died down she continued, "Thank you, everyone, for coming out to welcome me home. As you can tell, the surgery was a complete success and I cannot only speak but can completely hear, so for the first time I can hear my beautiful child and handsome husband speak. I can also hear all of your gorgeous voices." More clapping erupted and she waited for it to die down, smiling at everyone. "Of course, this just means I'm even more excited and driven to succeed in life because nothing can hold me back now. What I want to thank you for most of all is for not letting anything hold me back before. You never saw my disability as something that stopped me, and because of that it never did. Thank you, Andrew, for always having faith in me and now for giving me the ultimate gift. The ability to speak to you and to hear you speak to me. Thank you." She launched herself into his arms and wrapped her legs around him, kissing him deeply as everyone cheered again.

From there it was all about mingling from person to person; everyone wanted a chance to speak to her and hear what the surgery involved and what the therapy was like. Often she caught herself signing while she spoke and had to excuse herself. She said that was one of the greatest obstacles she struggled with and that she had to learn not to do that. She especially did it when excited or frustrated and angry or when she was thinking. On and on she explained, from one person to the next, but she found that she was getting tired and the noise was becoming too much. All the voices were starting to blend and Andrew must have sensed she was growing tired because he started to see people off. Maybe everyone sensed she needed rest; she didn't know why she felt disorientated. Dr. Kent explained that could happen from time to time in the beginning.

Heather excused herself from the party and went upstairs to their room to splash some water on her face. She could still hear whispers of the party floating up the stairs; one man particularly sounded angry, but she couldn't quite make out what he was saying. She thought maybe he was mad she had left suddenly, but then he must have left because she couldn't hear him anymore. She splashed her face again and walked out the room as Andrew came upstairs.

"You okay?" he asked.

"Yeah, just needed some air," she said. "Anyone still here?"

"No, Kyra's friends just left. Don't worry, I said goodbye for you; everyone understood that it was a bit much." He kissed her head softly and wrapped his arms around her. She leaned against him, resting her head on his chest softly.

"Was anyone annoyed that I left?" Heather asked softly. "Someone sounded annoyed."

"No, no one complained that I know of," Andrew said gently, stroking her back with his hand. "But Dr Kent said that you could get disorientated..."

"I know," Heather cut him off, "That's why I asked, just to make sure." She lifted her head. "I'm going to head to bed, okay? I want to get an early start at work tomorrow."

"I don't think you should go in tomorrow, babe, give it a few days."

"I've been off for weeks, Andrew. I need to get my head back in the game," Heather said with a note of finality.

Andrew nodded. "Okay, but if you don't feel well just promise me you'll come home and rest."

Heather nodded. "I promise."

They shared a soft kiss before Andrew left to check on Kyra and retrieve their lugged from the garage while Heather went back to the bedroom to get ready for bed.

~

Heather had never set the radio on her car and resolved to change the radio station when she got home from work. She didn't realize what garbage played in the morning every time she drove to work because, obviously, she couldn't hear it. However, if someone outside could they probably thought she had the most horrid taste ever. Now that she could hear she could get a USB device for her radio and load all her favorite music onto it.

She pulled into her parking bay at work and shut her car door, locking it and going towards the elevator. She couldn't believe how loud the city was. All the noises assaulted her as she drove to work and now, out of her car, it seemed worse somehow. She stepped onto the elevator and was amused by the silly music that played while she waited for it to reach her floor. The abrupt ding as it stopped at each floor to pick up more people was at first rather alarming, but she adjusted to it quickly. Everything seemed noisy even though no one was talking directly next to her; there seemed to be a general hum of noise that played throughout the building, through the walls. The sounds of machinery working, of footsteps, and very faintly of a few voices of people speaking in the distance.

When she reached her floor she excused herself and stepped off the elevator. She was greeted enthusiastically by everyone she passed and had to stop several times to chat to everyone who wasn't at the party at her house. Everyone wanted to hear her voice and to be honest, she wanted to hear theirs, to see if they sounded like she had imagined they would in her head. She wanted to laugh a lot of the time, and sometimes she did let out a giggle of excitement. By the time she reached her office she was an hour late and quickly got sucked into the work that Kayla had set on her table. The files were piled high and at first she thought it was just the usual going over the accounts and doing what she always did, but halfway through the stack Heather realized she didn't recognize some of the paperwork and buzzed for Kayla to come into her office.

"Yes, Heather," Kayla said as she walked in.

Heather held up some pink forms. "I haven't seen these before, what are these?"

"Oh, these are for closing accounts. Henry wants you to shut this client's down for good. They're no longer worthwhile dealing with so you have to call them and close their accounts," Kayla explained.

"I don't normally do this, it's not part of my job," Heather said.

"It is now that you're an account maintenance assistant. I mean I'm surprised they let me stay on with you since you're demoted; I guess they wanted to give you a chance to acclimatize," Kayla said.

"Demoted?" Heather asked, "What do you mean demoted?"

"You didn't know?" Kayla asked hesitantly. "I thought Henry emailed you and told you before you got back."

Heather reached for her computer, shoving the files aside. She scrolled through her emails before getting frustrated and simply sorting by name and looking for emails from Henry himself. She saw the one entitled **NEW ROLE** and clicked it. It detailed that since she was no longer 'disabled' and that she was on a level playing field with the other employees that she would be demoted and would have to work her way back up to a higher earning position. It was a legality, he called it, and hoped that it motivated her to do her absolute best. He would need her to clear out her office within two weeks of her being back. She would be assigned back to a cubicle and she would work under Wade.

The anger that Heather felt, and the betrayal, overwrote any sense of rational thought that she had. She couldn't believe that they thought all the hard work she had done meant nothing. That she only got her position in the company because she had been deaf. That nothing else she had done had meant anything. That they were going to set her back five years' worth of work and salary just because she could now hear and speak. To say she was upset was an understatement and Kayla could clearly sense Heather was about to explode because she left quickly, shutting the door behind her.

Heather picked up her phone and dialed Andrew, waiting impatiently for him to answer.

"These fucking bastards," she said, trying her best not to let the tears flow. "These fucking bastards demoted me to an account maintenance assistant, because basically I was only promoted because I was disabled."

"What?" Andrew said in disbelief. "They can't do that, babe."

"They have, it's done. All legal and everything," Heather said, taking a deep breath. "I have two weeks to empty out my office into a cubicle. I'll be working under Wade."

"Fuck that, you go tell Henry you quit," Andrew said. "Then come home and order your business cards and work out of the back office. Start your own company. You can do insurance from home;

you can apply for a loan from the bank and start your own thing."

"How?" Heather said.

"Be a broker for other insurance companies from home, you can do that," Andrew explained. "You're great at your job and you know what you're doing. Fuck Henry, you can start your own broker company."

Heather considered what Andrew was saying and realized he was being completely serious. She knew she had the skill to do it, and she certainly knew enough clients and the ins and outs of the business to take them with her. She knew the clients would follow her if she called them to. It was she, not the company, that the clients liked to work with after all.

"Okay," she said, "I'm quitting."

"You go, girl," Andrew said. "I'll see you at home."

"I love you, Andrew," Heather said.

"Love you too, babe," he responded before hanging up.

Heather stood up and walked out of her office and past Kayla. She felt empowered as she walked towards Henry's office. As she passed Wade's office he called to her, but she ignored him and continued along her way. She had nothing to say to him even when he stuck his head out of his office and called her name again. She continued and without knocking, she entered Henry's office.

Henry looked surprised to see her. "Heather, you need an appointment..." he started to say.

"I quit," she cut him off. "Effective immediately. I'll be collecting my things and leaving the building. I just wanted to let you know."

"You can't quit," Henry said, standing up. "Not after..."

"I can quit, I just did," Heather said with a smile before turning and walking out of Henry's office. He shouted after her, demanding she come back into his office, but she ignored him. Everyone turned to watch as she walked back to her office. Henry came out and started to berate her, but she didn't pay him any mind as she packed her things into a box. She didn't have many personal items so a small box suited her just fine. Wade came in to try and reason with Heather as well, but she wasn't having any of it. They had shown her what her worth was to the company, and now that she knew it, she was leaving for good.

She felt free.

Chapter Four

Once she arrived home the feeling of freedom felt a lot more like panic, but Heather took her things to the office out back and opened the door. The office was used as a storeroom and she'd have to empty it out, but she could do it. She started immediately, ignoring her phone as it rang constantly. She knew it was the office calling, but she didn't have time to nurture their bruised egos right now; she had work to do.

It took her three days to clear out the office of all the junk they had accumulated over the years. In the evenings she shopped online for furniture and other office supplies that arrived while she was cleaning. She set up shop and by Thursday she had a full office and was ready to start designing her logo, her business cards, and to have someone design her website for her.

She was nothing if not efficient. She named her business Lawrence Brokerage and her logo was done in a stunning blue to match Andrew and Kyra's eyes. Andrew funded everything without complaint and supported her every step of the way. She started calling up old customers of hers and offered to run their accounts, and she was pleased when over thirty percent of them started to consider switching to her and two major accounts told her to draw up the paperwork. She could imagine Henry seething already.

The only thing that bothered her was the constant chattering from her neighbor next door. It started early in the morning while she was having her coffee and went on throughout the day. It was almost as though he was on the opposite side of her office wall whispering to someone. It drove her absolutely mad. She brought it up with Andrew but as he pointed out, they couldn't very well tell their neighbors they couldn't talk in their own homes. Still, she tried to play music and even tried wearing earphones, but nothing drowned out the chatter.

It was really weird conversations as well. She couldn't make it out clearly, but she thought she heard them talk about blood and death and sacrifice. It sounded very macabre. Whatever they were talking about, specifically their male neighbor, spoke a lot and his voice droned on and on for hours.

"Cocksucker," she muttered and then stopped. She blushed crimson as it dawned on her she had actually said the word out loud. She never would have said something like that before. What had gotten into her? She shook her head and tried to clear her mind. It wasn't like her to use foul language, even if she was alone. She picked up the phone to call her husband then put it down again. She frowned. It was as though part of her wanted to call him and another part of her didn't want to, as though she was having a battle within herself. Giving herself another mental shake, she put it down to stress and got up and went to pour herself a cup of coffee from the machine she had bought for her office. She poured it and carried her cup back to her desk.

She sipped the coffee and pulled a face, realising she hadn't put any sugar or milk in it. It tasted... nice but odd. She normally preferred milk and sugar and yet the black coffee had a strange appeal to her.

Again it was like a small part of her had changed its taste in coffee. It was such a strange feeling, almost as though she didn't quite fit within herself. As though something was out, or off, or not quite there.

She got up and added milk and sugar to her coffee and settled down again, picking up her phone and calling Andrew. He didn't answer, but she left him a sweet voicemail about how much she loved him before she hung up the call.

She settled back into her desk and tried to ignore the chatting that had started again. It was one of the downsides of being able to hear now, the sounds distracted her whereas before she had been in blissful silence working undisturbed. When the chatting didn't stop, she decided that despite what Andrew said she had to do something about it. She got up and walked out of her office to the boundary wall. Strangely enough it didn't seem like the voices were louder outside than they were inside; she imagined they would be without the wall obstructing her from hearing them. She walked to the wall that separated their house and stood on her tiptoes to look over and into their neighbors' garden, but she didn't see anyone there. Still she could hear the chatting.

"Hello?" she called. The chatting stopped for a moment and she called again, "Hello?"

"No one's there, honey." Heather whipped around to face the opposite wall of her house to see her other neighbor, Louise, watering her garden.

"What do you mean no one's here?" she asked, walking across the yard to where Louise stood with hose in hand.

"They're on vacation, house is empty until next week," Louise explained.

"Oh," Heather exclaimed, "It's just I hear this constant chatting from the other side of the wall... You don't think someone's broken in, do you?" Heather paled.

Louise frowned and whipped out her cell phone. "We should call the police just in case."

While Louise dialed nine-one-one, Heather stood close by her, wondering if it was possible someone had broken into their neighbors' home and was staying there while the poor family was away. Heather didn't know those neighbors as well as she knew Louise, but she still wouldn't want anything bad to happen to their home.

"They're on their way," Louise said as she hung up the phone, "They'll be here in a few minutes and they said we mustn't approach the house or anyone that comes or goes from it. But if we see anyone, we must just take down a description of what they look like."

"Oh okay, I'm going to go inside and watch from the front room," Heather said.

"So am I," Louise said, turning the hose off and hurrying inside the house. Heather followed suit and went to her front room where she sat on the sofa and waited, watching out the front window for the police to arrive. All sorts of thoughts ran through her head from possible murderers to drug dealers, but she still felt excited to see if there was someone in the house and to see them get arrested.

When the police car showed up and the officers got out, Heather stayed back as Louise went out to speak to them. If there was someone in the house she didn't want them to know it was her who had been involved in reporting them. It may be selfish of her, but she didn't want to paint a target on her family.

As the officers went to the neighbors' house, Andrew arrived home and parked in the garage, watching the scene curiously as he did so. He walked into the house and saw Heather standing in the front room. "Hey babe, what's going on?"

"We think someone's broken in next door while the family is on vacation, so we called the cops just to check it out," she explained. "Louise told me the family's on vacation so it can't be them I'm hearing chatting away."

"Oh shit, hope everything is okay," Andrew said. "Are you okay?"

"Yeah, I'm fine, I didn't actually see anything..."

"No, I mean after the voicemail you left me," Andrew said.

"What do you mean?" Heather asked. "I thought that was a lovely voicemail."

"Uh, lovely isn't how I would describe that voice-mail, honey." He kissed her forehead. "Otherwise I wouldn't ask if you're okay. It was very unlike you to leave something like that on my phone."

Heather frowned, raising an eyebrow. "It's not lovely for me to leave a voicemail on my husband's phone about how much I love him?"

"Heather, do you remember what you said?" Andrew asked, taking his phone out and dialing his voicemail on speaker phone. Heather crossed her arms impatiently, but as she heard her own voice she balked at the words that were said.

"Hello, sexy beast, I can't wait until you get home later so I can ride that cock until you fill me with your cum like the little slut I am."

Heather glared at Andrew. "Is this a joke?" she asked. "How did you do that?"

"What are you on about, Heather? You left this on my phone."

"No, my voicemail was about how much I loved you and how I couldn't wait to see you later. Nothing sexual," Heather said through gritted teeth. "I wouldn't call myself a little slut Andrew; I have class."

Andrew held his phone out. "And you think I would for a laugh?"

Heather shook her head. "I didn't do it, Andrew, I know what I said."

"It's your voice, Heather," Andrew said. "It's here saved on my phone."

"I didn't say those things, Andrew," Heather said angrily, clenching her fists. "You know I wouldn't."

Andrew sighed and put his phone away, raising his arms and reaching out to hold Heather, but she pulled away. "I didn't do it, Andrew."

"I can't explain it, Heather," Andrew said. "I believe you though."

Heather relaxed a little and let Andrew pull her to him, wrapping his arms around her and rubbing her back. They stood like that for a moment before Andrew let her go so he could lean down and kiss her deeply. Heather returned the kiss, moaning softly into his mouth. Before they could go any further than that there was a knock at the door. Heather pulled away from Andrew and went to open the door to two police officers.

"Hi Mrs. Lawrence, your neighbor says that you were hearing people talking next door even though the family is away on vacation," the one officer said.

"Yes, that's right," Heather said, "It was a man, and they were talking about weird things like sacrifices and blood."

"It's probably just some teenagers messing around. We found no evidence of a break-in or cause for concern, but if you hear it again, here's our card you can just call us and we'll come immediately to patrol. We'll also keep a car patrolling the neighborhood regularly until the family is back."

"Thank you so much for coming out to check for us, Officer," Heather said with a smile.

"No problem, ma'am, you all have a good day now." With that the officers left and Heather set the card by the table with the phone where she would be able to find it again.

She went back to the front room where Andrew was now sitting on the sofa waiting for her. She smiled at him and said, "The officers said there's no sign of a break-in, so it's probably teenagers messing around."

"That's good at least," Andrew said. "At least it's nothing serious."

"At least," Heather said, moving to sit next to him on the sofa. "You know Kyra doesn't come home from school for another hour and a half..."

"I know," Andrew said as he flipped television channels, "I got off early today."

"Well, why don't we just forget all this nasty business of today and go have a nice, hot bath together and see where that leads to," Heather purred into his ear, leaning close to him so she could kiss his neck afterward.

Andrew shivered slightly and she could see goosebumps on his arm as she pulled away. Satisfied with the reaction, she got up and walked upstairs and heard his footsteps following her not too long after that. She drew them a hot bubble bath in the main bathroom and all too soon they were undressed and she was between his legs, resting with her back against him. This was the life for both of them. She couldn't think of a better way to spend the afternoon than laying naked against the man she loved, and she could tell he was enjoying it too from the way he caressed her skin and kissed her shoulder. She kept an eye on the time though, because she knew she wanted more than a simple bath out of this equation and it wasn't going to be in the bath because last time they tried that it was uncomfortable as hell.

"Do you like being able to make a noise now?" Andrew murmured.

"Hmmm?"

"When we have sex, do you like that you're able to make a noise now?" Andrew asked again, stroking his hand slowly down the side of her breast.

"I hadn't thought about it, but I know it's weird that I have to think about not making a noise when we're having sex in case we wake Kyra," she smiled, "We never had to worry about that before."

"We don't have to worry about that now," Andrew teased, sliding both his hands over her breasts and cupping them, giving them a gentle squeeze.

In a flurry of movements, and barely any drying, they tumbled out of the bath and into bed together, and Andrew was right; Heather didn't have to worry about keeping quiet this time so she didn't and she enjoyed it. She enjoyed being able to scream his name as he made her orgasm and she enjoyed hearing him call hers as he came inside of her.

And as they lay wrapped up in each other's arms afterward, her head resting against his warm chest and her breathing deep, she wondered if she would ever be able to have quiet sex again.

Chapter Five

"All I'm saying is that I think she can do better than B's and C's if she wants to go trick or treating this year," Heather said into the phone as she looked over the reports that had been emailed to her. She was on the phone with Andrew about Kyra's recent test results and she was less than impressed and knew the only way she was going to get through to her daughter was with something she loved. She was under a lot of stress, the business was growing quickly day by day, and with it she needed to hire staff. It didn't take a lot for her to convince Kayla to come and work for her; Kayla hated Henry anyway and wanted out of that company. Now she needed to start putting together a decent team to handle the accounts, but that would mean she would need office space soon. Andrew suggested getting a bigger house with more office space, but Heather had argued for getting an actual office, one with a board room where she could meet clients properly.

After much discussion and two more major accounts signing on, Heather got a small set of offices in the city and hired three employees to assist her. Things were going great and she couldn't believe how well she was doing. It was almost as though if she spoke something it would work well for her. Andrew always joked she'd sold her soul to the devil, but she thought she was just having a bout of good luck.

"Fucking dickhead," she said suddenly and stopped to look around to see if anyone had heard it. She didn't know what made her swear suddenly, but it wasn't the first time it had happened in the last few weeks.

"What happened?" Andrew asked.

"Kicked my toe," Heather lied, shifting the phone to her other ear and walking back out of her office and down the hallway. "It hurt a lot."

"Sorry, babe, but listen, I just don't think we should be too hard on Kyra right now; she has a lot going on."

"Everyone has a lot going on, Andrew. She can do better, and I don't think we should relax with her too much or she'll think it's acceptable behaviour. I know she is capable of doing fucking better than that." There was a pause of silence and Heather realized she had cursed again out loud. "Look, I'm sorry about the foul language, but I do know she can do better, don't you agree?"

Andrew sighed audibly into the phone and Heather wanted to reach through the handset and yank his vocal chords out through his throat. She paused, wondering where such a violent notion came from, especially for someone as peace loving as herself.

"She can do better, I agree. Okay, I'll talk to her," Andrew finally conceded.

"Thank you, that's all I ask. I'll chat to you later; I need to get these agreements in place, and I have a lunch date with Jeremy."

"Okay, baby," Andrew said, "I love you."

"You too," Heather said before hanging up.

She took the agreements to her office and set them on her table before grabbing her car keys and heading out the door.

"I'll see you in an hour or so, Kayla," Heather said.

"Whatever, you fat cunt,"

"Excuse me?" Heather asked aghast.

"I said, sure, Heather, I'll take messages," Kayla said, looking up curiously.

"Oh, I thought... I misheard... Sorry, yes, thank you. See you later," Heather stammered before she went to the elevator that would carry her down the floors of the building and towards the car park where her vehicle was. What had she thought she had heard? Kayla would never speak to her that way, not in a million years. Was she starting to hear things now? Maybe it was the stress getting to her.

She tried not to dwell on it as she pulled out of the car park and into the stream of steady traffic, heading into the city center and towards Jeremy. He had the day off from his new job and had been so glad to hear from Heather when she had sent him a text to suggest they meet up so they could catch up with the latest of what was going on in the deaf community. Heather had been surprised at how much she missed her community now that she was no longer a part of it and wanted to see if she could still contribute to it. She found a parking spot, which was another stroke of luck in her books as there was never any parking this side of town, and she locked her car and headed to the little cafe where she was meeting Jeremy.

Jeremy was already seated with two coffees in front of him, waiting for her. He saw her walk in and instinctively waved for her attention then realized he could call her.

"Heather, Heather, here!" he squealed and so did she as she reached him, ignoring the strange looks they got from the other patrons. They hugged tightly for a while before tumbling into their seats.

"Tell me everything!" Jeremy said.

Heather grinned. "The surgery was obviously a success so I can hear and speak now, and it's just the most amazing thing ever, Jeremy. I quit with Henry and started my own company that is doing absolutely great; we have so many clients on board already that I even have my own offices now." On and on she went telling Jeremy every detail of what had happened since he had last seen her.

Jeremy listened attentively and was so wrapped up in the conversation that it took them both a moment to realize that their coffees were getting cold. This made them both burst out laughing and they ordered fresh ones before continuing the conversation.

"I just can't believe it; you have such a beautiful voice, exactly as I imagined it in my head when I was interpreting for you," Jeremy said.

"Thank you, it took some getting used to. Even now I sometimes just like to talk out loud just to hear it," Heather said blushing slightly. "I know it's weird, but after spending so long in silence it's such a change."

"Oh, I can imagine," Jeremy said. "Now I'm going to nip to the little boys' room before I tell you everything about my new job and then I want to tell you about this new meet and greet at the deaf club that you have to come to. I don't care that you can hear now; you still have to come. Give me two seconds." He stood up and walked off and Heather stirred sugar into her new coffee while she waited.

She couldn't stop smiling as she sipped her brew, thinking about how many times she had wanted to 'say' something to Jeremy and now she could.

She was so wrapped up in her own happiness that it took her a moment to realize that there was a really angry conversation happening next to her. Two men were fighting at the table next to hers, their voices getting louder and louder. Everyone else had stopped what they were doing to look at the men awkwardly, and it seemed the waitresses were arguing over who they were sending over to quell the argument.

"I'll kill you, you son of a bitch," the one man screamed. "I'll shoot you dead for what you've done to me and my wife."

"You're a coward, you haven't got the balls to shoot anyone."

"You think so? You think I don't have the balls?"

Jeremy slipped back into his chair and looked over at Heather. "Jeez, what do you think they're arguing about?"

"I don't know, but it escalated quickly," Heather said.

"What?" Jeremy asked, "What language is that?"

"What do you mean?" Heather asked looking at him curiously.

"Heather, stop joking around, when did you learn a foreign language? Can you understand them?"

"I don't know what you're talking about, Jeremy?" Heather said, sitting straight, "I'm speaking English to you."

Jeremy frowned and could see the concern on Heather's face, so he said, "Heather, you do know you're speaking whatever those guys are speaking, right? Like Greek or Italian or something... Sweetie, are you okay?"

"No, no, I'm not okay. I don't speak foreign languages," Heather said. "Jeremy, this isn't funny, stop making a joke out of this."

Jeremy reached a hand across the table and touched hers lightly. "Calm down, sweetie, I don't understand a word of what you're saying," Jeremy said. "Come on, let's get out of here. Maybe that will help." He stood and put some cash on the table.

Heather stood and kept trying to talk to him. "Jeremy, the guy, he said he's going to shoot the other guy. Maybe we should call the cops. Do you understand? This isn't a joke. I'm not playing around with this."

"Heather, sweetie, I don't understand you, slow down," Jeremy said, putting an arm around her, "Just calm down, obviously something is wrong and it's triggered something and you're speaking a foreign language. Let's just get you home and safe and we can see what's…"

They were a few steps out of the cafe when the gunshots behind them made them drop to the floor, screaming in terror. Another single shot went off making them scream once more, and everyone around them started running, trampling over each other in their panicked state to get away. Jeremy did his best to cover Heather and protect her from the various runners and once able to, he got her up and moving as fast as she could away from the cafe.

Once a safe distance away, he checked her over for any gunshots before calling the police. "Hello, yes, there's been shots fired at Little Tony's Cafe. I don't know, we just heard the shots and ran. No, I don't think we're hurt, but there might be someone who is. Please, can you send the police and an ambulance? You're speaking to Jeremy Christophers. Yes, ma'am, I'm at the corner of Fifth Avenue and Jones Road. I'll wait for the police. Yes, ma'am. Thank you."

"Are they coming?" Heather asked.

"Yes, they are," Jeremy said hugging her tightly, "Thank God you're okay."

"I was trying to tell you, those men who were fighting, the one threatened to shoot the other one."

"I couldn't understand you, Heather, you were speaking a different language," Jeremy said. "Honestly, I don't know what you were speaking, but it wasn't English."

Heather teared up. "I could have stopped it from happening."

"Oh sweetie, it's not your fault," Jeremy said, hugging her again. "It's nobody's fault but the shooter."

"How was I talking a foreign language though? How is that possible?" Heather asked.

"I don't know, honey; we'll have you checked out by the ambulance, but you should consult with your doctor. It could be nothing, but it could be something serious," Jeremy said, taking her hand. "Got to make sure you're okay, okay?"

Heather nodded. "Okay, I need to let Andrew know what's happened, along with the office. I'll be back now."

Jeremy nodded and kept an eye on her as she trailed off a little to phone Andrew and the office and let them know where she was and what had happened. After assuring Andrew a few times that she was okay and safe, she finally managed to call the office and let them know that she wasn't going to be back for the remainder of the day. By the time she was done on both calls, the police were on the scene and Jeremy was talking to two detectives outside the cafe.

"So he shot himself after shooting the guy he was talking to?" Jeremy asked

"Seems like it," the detective said, "You say your friend knew what was going to happen but had some sort of mental break?"

"It wasn't a mental break," Heather said as she approached them, "I just couldn't communicate to Jeremy what was being said. He said I was speaking a foreign language, but to me I was speaking English."

"And you don't speak any foreign languages naturally?" the detective asked.

"Up until a few weeks ago, I wasn't able to speak at all, Detective," Heather said. "I was deaf and mute until recently, when I had corrective surgery. Jeremy thinks I was speaking the same language that the men were arguing in, but I don't know any other language aside from sign language and English."

"You should have yourself checked out, ma'am," the one detective said, "just to be on the safe side."

"I will, was anyone else hurt?" she asked worriedly.

"No, it seemed they were having an argument over something and the one gentleman shot the other gentleman and then himself. That's all the details we have for now until we move further into our investigation."

"At least no one else was hurt," Heather said, hugging herself, "Can we go?"

"First, go get yourselves checked out by the ambulance and then you're free to go, but leave your contact details with the officers in case there are any follow-up questions."

"We will, thank you," Jeremy said.

They made their way over to a uniformed police officer and gave him their contact details before going to wait their turn by the ambulance. Jeremy explained the situation to the paramedic before getting checked out and then Heather sat down to get checked out.

"So you really don't know any foreign languages and you just started speaking one today?" the paramedic asked.

"Apparently," Heather said, "That's what everyone is telling me."

"I recommend you get a head CT from the hospital, just to be sure; there isn't much we can check here in terms of scans and I'd rather be safe than sorry. Here's the details of a good neurologist at the closest hospital. Can your friend take you?"

"Yes, I can," Jeremy said, "I don't want her driving there by herself either."

"I'll have to call Andrew," Heather said, "Let him know what's happening."

"You can call him while I drive you," Jeremy said. "I caught a taxi here so we'll take your car."

She gave him the keys and they thanked the paramedic before heading off towards her car.

"I hope it's nothing serious," Heather said as she buckled into the passenger side of her car.

"I'm sure it isn't, it's probably something really logical, but let's rather get peace of mind now."

Heather dialed Andrew's number.

"Hey baby, are you okay?" Andrew asked.

"Yeah, but I have to go to St. Joseph's for a head scan. Can you meet me there? I think grab a taxi so you can take my car home."

"Why do you need a scan? What happened? I thought you weren't shot." She could hear the worry in his voice.

"I wasn't shot, but they just want to make sure everything is okay with my head. I'll explain everything when you get there, but it's really nothing to stress about, love, I promise."

"I'll get Louise to watch Kyra and I'll be on my way," Andrew said, "Love you."

"Love you too."

Chapter Six

"Heather Lawrence," the nurse called and Heather perked up. She had been in the waiting room for over an hour. Jeremy had left when Andrew arrived and had taken over watching her. She had dozed off a few times in the waiting room, bored from doing nothing, and when they finally called her name she was startled awake.

Andrew chuckled softly and she smacked his arm. "Oh hush," she said, standing up.

"We're ready for you," the nurse said, leading her into an examination room. "The doctor will be with you shortly."

Heather climbed onto the bed and waited while Andrew stood awkwardly to the side, not sure what to do with himself. It wasn't long before an elderly gentlemen walked in. "Good day, Mrs. Lawrence, I'm Dr. Carson and I'll be treating you today. Now you're here for a head CT after a shooting incident, is that correct?"

"Correct, but it's what happened before the incident that has us worried," Heather explained.

"And what was that?" the doctor asked, taking a seat on a stool and getting out his paperwork to make notes.

"Well, I heard the two men arguing, and when I went to tell my friend about the argument, I was apparently speaking a foreign language. I don't know any foreign languages. He said it sounded like Greek or Italian."

"And you've never studied these languages before in your life?"

"No, in fact up until a few weeks ago, I couldn't hear or speak. I was part of a trial for a surgery for deaf and mute people to enable them to speak and hear again by transplanting vocal chords and cochlear parts. It's in my medical history, I can have it sent over."

"I've heard of trials like this; it's very risky but apparently a good success with you," Dr. Carson said. "However, with every surgery there is a risk so let's send you down for a CT and make sure there's nothing wrong."

"What could it possibly be?" Andrew asked. "Could it be something from the surgery?"

"There is no point in speculating until we have the scans, Mr. Lawrence. I suggest you go to the cafeteria and get some coffee. We'll take good care of your wife."

Andrew sighed and kissed Heather softly before walking out the room. Dr. Carson gave her a hospital gown to don and told her where she could leave her clothes and belongings while she went for the scans. After ensuring she was settled in, he left, promising that some nurses would be in to assist her shortly.

Heather looked around the sterile room nervously. She never used to be nervous about hospitals, but this made her nervous. She knew there would be risks when she agreed to have the surgery, but what if she had something seriously wrong with her brain now and they had to reverse the surgery? She didn't think she could go back to a world of silence now that she had heard all the beautiful sounds and had a voice of her own to speak with. The thought terrified her.

A male nurse came in and smiled at her. "Hi, Mrs. Lawrence, I'm Tucker and I'm going to take you down to your CT." He pulled up a wheelchair for her to get into. "You can just take a seat here for me. I know you can walk, but hospital protocol is that I push you around in this so you don't get hurt on my watch."

Heather smiled at him. "Hi Fucker," she said and then blushed crimson. "I'm sorry, I don't know why I said that. I meant to say 'hi Tucker.'"

"It's okay, Mrs. Lawrence, I believe we're checking your head out today so it's all good."

Heather kept her mouth shut the whole way down to the CT section, not trusting herself to speak another word. She couldn't believe she had slipped like that. She had never been so rude to someone before and she was utterly embarrassed. Tucker still spoke to her calmly and professionally, as though nothing had happened, but she simply nodded as they went along. As he was helping her up onto the machine for the CT scan she suddenly blurted out, "Fuck shit this motherfucker!" She slapped a hand against her mouth and shook her head, tears forming in her eyes.

Tucker looked at her worriedly. "Are you okay, Mrs. Lawrence? Did I hurt you?"

"No, I just… I didn't want to say anything; that just came out by itself."

Tucker patted her on the back. "You go on and lay down now and get as comfortable as you can; try not to move. I'm going to make some notes in your chart for the doctor."

Heather took a few deep breaths and laid down, trying not to let the tears threatening to spill take over. Once the scans started she did her best not to move, but her mind was racing over what could possibly be wrong with her. Was it cancer? A tumor on her brain? Was this her punishment for all the good she had experienced of late? Was this the balance of it? Was she going to die?

She suddenly felt claustrophobic, but before she could say anything, the scans were done and they were pulling her out and helping her back into the wheelchair. She shivered as though the air around her was ice cold and the nurse noticed.

"Are you okay, honey?" he asked.

"I'm just cold," she said, hugging herself.

"We'll get you back to your room and get you dressed and warmed up again," Tucker said, pushing her along.

Heather continued to shiver uncontrollably as they went along and Tucker watched her like a hawk. Once back in her room, he pulled the curtain around her bed so she could get dressed while they waited for the doctor.

Heather sat on the bed again, waiting for the doctor to come in. She heard the door open and close and pulled the curtain back to see Andrew had come back in.

"Hey baby, everything go okay?" he asked, bringing her a cup of coffee.

Heather took it gladly and sat back in the bed as they waited for the doctor to come back. It was an awkward silence that they fell into as they waited, and Andrew hovered nervously around the bed.

When the door opened, they both turned to see Dr. Carson walk in with scans in his hand. "Mrs. Lawrence, there seems to be nothing wrong with your brain that we can see from the scans, so I can only deduce that it could be a psychological effect of the surgery that you underwent." Dr. Carson put the scans up against a light box to show her. "Everything appears to be normal and functioning as it should, so you have nothing to worry about from a physical aspect."

Heather let out a sigh of relief and smiled at Dr. Carson. "So what could it be then?"

"More than likely it's a psychological reaction, so I'm going to refer you to a good doctor here in the city; you can make an appointment any time to go and see him," Dr. Carson said, making notes on his notepad. "But as far as I'm concerned you're as fit as a fiddle."

Heather smiled and slipped off the examination table and took the paper from the doctor. "Thank you so much, Dr. Carson; that is reassuring to know there's nothing physically wrong with me."

"Thank you, Dr. Carson," Andrew said as he held the door open for Heather to walk through. He took her hand and they went to the front desk to finish up her paperwork before she could leave. Once they were done there, they walked out of the hospital together and Heather let out another big sigh of relief.

"Well, thank goodness there's nothing wrong with my brain."

"Well, not physically, but I still want you to go to this psychologist and see what's cooking in that mind of yours," Andrew said.

"I will," Heather said calmly. "But it's still a relief that I don't need like brain surgery or something."

"I know, baby, I know," Andrew said, putting an arm around her shoulders as they walked together.

The wind picked up around them. It was starting to get cooler as the months moved towards fall. The trees were changing color and losing their leaves, and Andrew knew it would soon be time for warmer drinks and roaring fires in the fireplace. For now though, he was just happy that Heather was safe and healthy. He opened the car door for her and let her climb into the passenger side before shutting the door for her. He then went to the driver's side and climbed in.

Once buckled in, he started the car and began to drive towards their home, letting her music fill the silence between them.

"I'm not saying you're crazy," Andrew said as he diced tomatoes for their dinner, "I'm just saying that going to the head doctor would put your mind at ease."

"And I'm just saying that now that it is all over and done it was a once-off thing and I'd like to put it behind me," Heather said. She had thought about it the whole car ride home and had finally concluded that it was stress. Starting the new company combined with the surgery and everything else that had happened was just taking its toll on her. She had googled on her phone about cases where people could suddenly speak foreign languages and there were documented cases where trauma could cause people to suddenly develop the ability to speak a different language.

"Google doesn't know everything," Andrew said. "You can't just search for answers on the Internet and interpret them the way you want to; you are not a doctor."

"It makes sense though, doesn't it?" Heather said, putting her hands on her hips. "Tell me it doesn't make sense, Andrew."

Andrew sighed and ran a hand over his face. "All I'm saying is getting a professional..."

"It does make sense, you just want me to waste money getting a professional doctor to say what I already know is right." Heather was exasperated.

"What are you guys arguing about this time?" Kyra asked as she walked in with her headphones around her neck, "I can hear you over my music."

"Honey, what have I told you about prolonged use of those things? You're going to damage your hearing," Heather said, reaching to take her headphones off.

Kyra dodged her mother and stole a tomato from the cutting board, popping it in her mouth with a satisfied smile. "So are you crazy, Mom?"

"See, now look at what you've started, Andrew; now the child thinks I'm insane." Heather turned back to her husband.

"Mom isn't crazy, Kyra, don't rile her up, please. I'm having a hard enough time trying to convince her to go see the doctor without you meddling in it," Andrew said, throwing the tomatoes into the salad. "And why the sudden change of heart, Heather? You were all for going to the doctor when we were at the hospital."

"I just don't want to when I know my own body and mind, and I know what the logical explanation is," Heather said, reaching into the bowl and stealing a tomato as well.

"Thieves, the lot of you," Andrew proclaimed.

The girls both giggled and left him to finish making the salad as they went to set the dinner table. Heather smiled at Kyra as she set the plates down at their places. "How is school?" she asked.

"Dad spoke to me already, Mom. I know you want me to do better," Kyra said.

"It's because I know you can do better, Kyra," Heather said. "I know what you're capable of."

Kyra didn't answer her back; she simply set the glasses in their places and went back to the kitchen to get the cutlery. Heather sighed softly and straightened everything out, pausing only when she heard a glass shatter, "What was that?" she called.

"What was what?" Andrew called back.

"I heard a glass break," Heather said, walking back into the kitchen.

Kyra was standing by the cutlery drawer and Andrew was still by the salad, tossing the ingredients together.

"I didn't hear anything. Kyra?" he asked.

"No, I didn't hear a glass break." Kyra shrugged.

"I'm sure I heard a glass shatter," Heather said. "I can't be sure where though."

"Kyra, go check your room," Andrew said, setting the salad spoons down. "I'll go check the rest of the house. Heather, why don't you check the front of the house? Be careful you don't cut yourself on anything."

They separated and walked throughout the house. Heather looked everywhere, checking the windows were closed while she was at it, but she found no sign of anything that was broken. When they met back in the kitchen, Andrew shrugged. "Might have been at the neighbors," he said.

"Maybe," Heather said, unsettled. "My hearing must be really good."

"Remind me never to whisper anything under my breath," Kyra joked, trying to lighten the mood.

Andrew smiled at her and said, "Right. Everyone to the dining room; it's time for dinner, please."

Heather and Kyra went to the dining room. Heather carried a plate of rolls and Kyra took a pitcher of fruit juice with her. Andrew brought through the dish of lasagna and then went back to retrieve the salad before they all settled down for dinner. They didn't speak much as they ate, comfortable in the silence that settled amongst them. Heather couldn't shake the feeling, though, about the shattered glass; it had definitely sounded as though it was inside the house.

Once they were finished eating and had tidied up, they went upstairs to get ready for bed. Lying in bed, Heather replayed the shattered glass over in her mind; she was sure it had come from inside the house and as Andrew dozed off peacefully next to her, she couldn't shake the feeling that something was wrong. She tossed and turned and tried to get comfortable but she just couldn't fall asleep.

She sat up in bed and strained to hear if anything else sounded off. She got up and went to check on Kyra, who was fast asleep in bed; she tucked her in and hugged herself before going back to her own bed. She couldn't shake the feeling as though someone was watching her. She climbed back into bed and snuggled up to Andrew, chiding herself for such thoughts. With Andrew's arms wrapped around her, she finally managed to fall into a fitful sleep.

Chapter Seven

"He is coming up for a few weeks to check on several patients so I have made an appointment to go see him," Heather said as she sipped her coffee. She was seated at the table. It was a beautiful Saturday fall morning and Andrew, still looking tired from having just woken up, was seated opposite her with a cup of coffee as well.

"He flew from Mexico just to check on his patients, that's awfully nice of him," Andrew commented, trying to stifle a yawn. "When do you see him?"

"Today, at midday, he has rented some offices in town for while he is here. He'll be here until after Halloween and then he flies back," Heather explained as Kyra came bouncing downstairs.

"Morning," Kyra said, "I've made a decision."

"It's too early for decisions," Andrew grumbled into his coffee as Kyra kissed his head.

"I want to dress as a techno-witch for Halloween this year," Kyra explained. "It's like a musical witch. A DJ witch if you will."

"Of course you do, honey," Heather said with a smile. "I bet it involves your headphones in some shape or manner."

"It does," Kyra confirmed. "I made it up myself." She went to the kitchen to make her cereal.

"That's your child," Andrew said. "Without a doubt, that is your child."

"I know, isn't it lovely," Heather gushed, giggling.

Kyra came back to sit at the table to eat her cereal. "So can we go get my costume today, Mom? I have some ideas."

"I have a doctor appointment today, but if you go with me, we can go afterward," Heather said. "Then we can also grab some Halloween decorations and candy for the night. Does Dad know what he is going as for Halloween yet?" They both looked at Andrew.

"A dentist," Andrew mumbled. "A murder dentist," he added.

"You joke, but that's what I'll pick up for you," Heather said with a smile.

"Do it. I'll totally be a murder dentist," Andrew said, smiling cheekily. "Who doesn't want to see a dentist on the night they eat all the candy?"

"What about you, Mom? What are you going to be?"

Heather stared into her coffee and then said, "I think I'll go as a vampire this year."

Both Andrew and Kyra groaned and Heather looked up. "What?"

"You go as a vampire every year; pick something different," Andrew said.

"Like what? A nurse?" Heather teased. "A vampire suits me."

"Mom, you could be anything on Halloween; that's the point. Vampires are boring. Lola's mom is going as a mummy. Get it? A mummy!" Kyra giggled at the thought and Andrew chuckled.

Heather smiled and said, "I don't know, a vampire is my go to. What would you guys have me go as?"

Andrew and Kyra smiled at each other, and Kyra got up and went to Andrew so they could huddle together and whisper to each other. Heather laughed at how ridiculous they looked and sipped her coffee, waiting patiently for them to come to a decision. When they finally broke up their little team meeting, Kyra stood up straight and said, "We've decided you should dress as the devil, Mom."

"The devil?" Heather asked.

"Yes, the devil, dear," Andrew chuckled, "Satan himself."

"But that's a boy costume," Heather protested.

"Come on, Mommy," Kyra said, throwing her arms around Heather and nearly knocking her coffee out of her hands.

"Careful now, Kyra," she said, looking into her daughter's eyes. "The devil, huh? Mistress of evil is what I should go as?"

"Yes," Kyra said, planting a kiss on her mother's cheek.

"Okay, fine, if I agree to go as the devil then Dad has to agree to go as an evil dentist," Heather said.

"Deal," Andrew said, "You can pick out my costume." Andrew set his coffee down. "Now you two better get up and dressed and ready if you're going to go to the appointment and then go spend all my money on Halloween stuff."

"Can we get pumpkins to carve?" Kyra asked, going back to her cereal.

"Sure, we can, honey, although you know Daddy will out carve both of us as usual." Heather grinned.

"It's not my fault I'm an engineer," Andrew pointed out, getting up to take his coffee cup to the dishwasher.

Heather smiled. "Finish your breakfast and get dressed; we need to go into town for the appointment once I'm finished cleaning the house."

"Okay, Mommy," Kyra said.

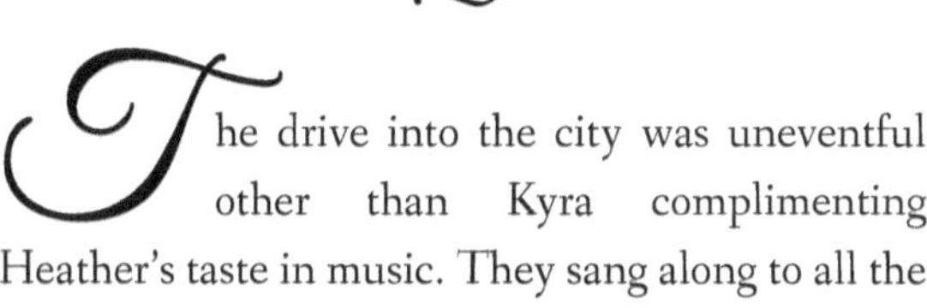

The drive into the city was uneventful other than Kyra complimenting Heather's taste in music. They sang along to all the songs that played in the car, turning the volume up as loud as possible and singing their hearts out. When they finally arrived at the offices, Heather turned the volume down and found a parking bay.

They walked into the offices and went to reception where a red haired nurse was sitting typing at a computer.

"Hi, I'm Heather Lawrence, here to see Dr. Kent for a check-up," Heather said as she reached the desk.

"Please take a seat," the nurse said, indicating the chairs to the left side of the room. Heather took Kyra's hand and went to sit down. Kyra wriggled her hand free and put her headphones on, playing on her phone as they waited for their appointment. Heather looked at her watch and noted they were on time, so they shouldn't wait too long if the doctor was running according to schedule.

"Mrs. Lawrence," Dr. Kent said as he strode out of an office behind the nurses' station, "Please, this way."

Heather tapped Kyra and said, "Stay here, don't go anywhere." Kyra nodded that she understood and

Heather smiled, following Dr. Kent into his examination room.

"Is everything well? Nothing is wrong I hope?" Dr. Kent questioned as he indicated she could get on the examination table.

Heather set her things down on a chair and climbed onto the table and while Dr. Kent started to examine her, she said, "Everything is fine; I don't get headaches anymore and my throat doesn't ache if I talk for extended periods. There was, however, an incident..."

"An incident? Tell me about it," Dr. Kent said.

"Well, a while ago a friend and I were at a cafe and some guys were arguing in a foreign language and I understood them, and when I tried to explain it to my friend he couldn't understand me because suddenly, I was speaking a foreign language. I've read that it's possible for that to happen with traumatic cases so I put it down to stress."

"You're referring to Foreign Accent Syndrome," Dr. Kent said, "Although rare, it would make sense in such a case. We did operate which is traumatic in a sense so yes, logically that could happen I suppose."

"I told my husband as such," Heather said. "He wanted me to go get all sorts of tests done, but it was so logical I didn't think it was necessary."

"Well, I can imagine he is worried about you after coming out of an extensive surgery like the one you've had. Have there been any other incidents?" Dr. Kent asked curiously.

"No, well, kind of..." Heather blushed slightly, "I'm rather embarrassed to say but sometimes I feel as though I hear things that aren't there, and sometimes I blurt out things I don't mean to say. Things quite unlike me."

"Interesting," Dr. Kent said. "Turn your head." He examined her ears thoroughly and then sat back. "Well, your hearing is keen so it's possible you're hearing things from far away and just misjudging how close they are."

"That's what Andrew says as well, but I swear they sound like they're right by me," Heather says. "Like glasses shattering or sometimes people say one thing but then say they said another thing."

"That could just be stress, your brain mixing up signals. Nothing to worry about just yet, but we'll keep an eye on it. As for blurting out things, that's just something to get used to. You're not used to being able to suddenly say things and now you can; it will just take time and adjustment. There is one final thing I want to tell you before you go and then we can sign you out."

"Okay," Heather said, "What's that?"

Dr. Kent smiled and sat back, speaking in a dark and mysterious voice, "Expergisci."

"**Mom!** Mom! Hello! Earth to Mom!"

Heather blinked a few times and looked around. They were standing in the middle of the Halloween section of the store and Kyra was waving her hand in front of Heather's face.

"How...how did we get here?" Heather asked.

"What do you mean? We've been here almost an hour shopping; we've been to two different shops already," Kyra said.

"I...I was just speaking to Dr. Kent and I... How did we come here? I don't remember leaving his office." Heather shivered slightly, looking at her watch and trying to recall the events between when she was at Dr. Kent's office and now. It was a total blank.

"Are you okay, Mom?" Kyra asked looking at her worriedly. "Should I call Dad?"

"No, no," Heather said, running a hand over her face. "No, I just...I blanked out is all." She smiled at Kyra. "What do we have left to get? Where are we exactly in our shopping?"

"We were just getting Dad's costume and the pumpkins and we were done," Kyra said hesitantly. "Are you sure you're okay? You've been kind of spacey since we left the doctor's office."

"I'm fine, sweetheart," Heather said. "Come, let's find Dad's things and get those pumpkins and head home so we can carve."

Kyra eyed her but didn't say anything further as they walked the aisles picking out the necessary parts of Andrew's costume. After that they headed to the produce section and picked out three monstrous sized pumpkins to carve for Halloween before heading to the checkout. All the while Heather kept trying to recall the events that led to them heading to the shops. She remembered everything up until Dr. Kent saying he wanted to tell her one last thing before she could sign out, and after that everything simply went blank. She couldn't explain it. It was as though she had left her body and simply hadn't been there for the last two hours. How had she driven? With Kyra in the car on top of everything. Had they talked and what about? She noticed Kyra still looking at her worried, so she gave her a small smile.

"Why don't we get pumpkin spiced lattes on our way out from the coffee shop for the ride home, my wicked techno witch from the west?" she offered.

Kyra gave her a hesitant smile. "Okay, Mommy."

She put a reassuring arm around her daughter as they pushed their shopping cart through the check out and had everything wrung up. Heather paid for it with Andrew's card before loading it all back into the cart and leading Kyra out the store and towards the coffee shop next door. They joined the line outside and waited for their turn; Kyra putting her headphones on to listen to music while they waited gave Heather a chance to try and collect herself again. She was worried about telling Andrew about blanking out like that. He would worry, especially since she had Kyra with her. What if she had an accident or caused an accident? What if Kyra had gotten hurt? She would never forgive herself.

"Two pumpkin spiced lattes, please?" she asked the barista as she reached the front of the line. She paid for the drinks and handed Kyra hers before they set off for the car. She let Kyra lead the way since she couldn't even remember where she had parked. No, she wouldn't tell Andrew about this incident. He wouldn't feel that Kyra was safe with her. Maybe she would call Dr. Kent and ask him what happened in the office; maybe he could shed some light. That was the best plan of action she could come up with.

They loaded the car and put the cart away before climbing in and driving home. Heather let Kyra turn the music up full blast so they could sing to it as they drove and although everything appeared normal, Heather couldn't help the feeling of dread that bubbled inside of her.

~

"Did you buy everything in the shop or did you leave some things for other people?" Andrew asked as they parked the car in the garage.

"We left some stuff for other people, I guess," Kyra teased, giggling as she opened the trunk of the car and grabbed some of the shopping bags.

"You coming, honey?" Andrew called to Heather.

"Coming," Heather called back as she watched him and Kyra carry some of the bags into the house, joking about how many there were. Heather climbed out of the car and went into the house, going upstairs to her bathroom to wash her face. She splashed cool water on herself and stared at her reflection; she looked slightly haggard and tired but otherwise, everything looked normal. She stared into her own eyes for what felt like an eternity, until in her reflection she saw big hairy legs climb out of her right ear and pull a big hairy spider's body out after them.

Heather screamed and beat at her ear, trying to get the spider off of her. Andrew came running in. "What is it?" he shouted.

Heather curled up on the floor sobbing, "There was a spider in my ear, a giant spider."

"What? Where?" Andrew pulled Heather off the floor and into his arms, looking around her. Kyra hovered at the door, afraid to come in because of the spider and also afraid to come in because of her mother. Andrew rocked Heather against him, stroking her back gently. He glanced at Kyra. "Go make Mom a strong cup of tea; we'll be down now."

Kyra nodded and left her parents in the bathroom, leaving her father to calm her mother down. Heather pulled away from Andrew and wiped her eyes on the backs of her hands. "I thought I saw a spider crawl out of my ear, it freaked me out."

"So was there a spider?" Andrew asked.

"I don't know, I thought so, but maybe it was just my mind playing tricks on me again," Heather said, hugging herself.

"Are you okay, babe? What did Dr. Kent say?" Andrew reached up and stroked her hair softly.

"He said I checked out perfectly, that it's just stress and I need to take it easy," Heather lied, wiping her eyes again. "Maybe I'll take a few days off of work, just relax a little," she added.

"Good idea," Andrew said. "Why don't you come and have your cup of tea and relax a little now? We'll take out all that stress on those pumpkins."

"Okay," Heather said, following Andrew downstairs. She glanced back once at the mirror and shivered, before shutting the bathroom door.

Chapter Eight

Heather stirred fitfully from her sleep. She didn't know what it was that was waking her, but something was disturbing her rest. She sat up in bed and tilted her head to the side sleepily. It had been two days since the spider incident. Something had woken her and she couldn't place her finger on what it was. As her mind cleared from its sleepy fog, she realized that she was hearing a thudding noise and a man talking. Suddenly gripped by fear, she shook Andrew awake.

"Andrew, there's someone in the house," Heather whispered.

"What?" Andrew said, sitting up in bed.

Heather climbed out of bed, worried about Kyra. She slipped into her slippers and gown and went to check on her daughter without another thought of herself. As she reached Kyra's door the thudding got louder and she worried that it was coming from Kyra's room. She opened the door to find Kyra sound asleep. Heather walked into the room and looked around but found nothing and couldn't hear the noise anymore. Andrew came into the room with a baseball bat in one hand, looking half-awake in his boxer shorts.

"I swear I heard someone; check the house," Heather whispered, "I'll stay here with Kyra."

Andrew nodded, now waking up and more alert, he gripped the bat with both hands and walked out into the hallway and went to check the rest of the house. Heather waited anxiously for him to return and when he did, she sighed with relief.

"There's no one else here, babe, and everything is still locked up," he whispered.

Heather nodded and hugged herself. "Sorry," she said, walking to him and letting him wrap an arm around her shoulders and guide her back to bed. As they reached the bedroom Heather glanced at their mirror and saw their reflections. What struck her was next to her face appeared the face of another man who suddenly spoke to her in a weird language, causing her to scream and jump into Andrew.

"What? What is it?" Andrew asked, looking around.

"In the mirror!" Heather exclaimed.

Andrew turned the light on. "What's in the mirror?" he said looking in the direction of their mirror and seeing nothing out of the ordinary.

Heather peeked between her fingers and saw nothing but their reflections and felt instantly foolish for screaming like she had. She rubbed her eyes and said, "I thought I saw...and I heard... Babe, I'm not losing my mind; there was a face and it spoke..."

"Love, you're probably still half asleep from a bad nightmare and seeing shit. You really shouldn't watch so much television before bed," Andrew chuckled, setting the bat down and turning the light off again.

Heather blushed crimson and climbed back into bed, snuggling close to Andrew and letting him wrap his arms around her securely. "I'm sorry, love, I don't know what's wrong with me."

"No more midnight snacks and television before bedtime," Andrew said through a yawn.

Heather was tempted to glance at the mirror again but thought better of it. Shutting her eyes, she simply breathed in Andrew's scent and curled up against him to go back to sleep.

~

Heather woke up more exhausted than rested, as though she had spent the night tossing and turning in her sleep. She didn't feel like she had slept at all. Every night there were strange noises that kept waking her and she didn't want to wake Andrew every time she thought she heard something go bump in the night or he'd be up all night with her. She'd get up and try to find the source of the noise, but she couldn't. It ranged from a thudding noise to whispering voices to glass shattering to high pitched whining. Heather was starting to believe that maybe she was losing her mind after all and she was imagining all the noises. It didn't just happen the one night either, it happened every night of the week, and the exhaustion started to show as dark circles formed under her eyes and she struggled to stay awake during the day. She couldn't concentrate on what was going on around her and it didn't help trying to nap during the day because the noises woke her up then too.

Andrew had noticed the change in his wife and had begged her to make an appointment to see Dr. Kent, but she couldn't get an appointment until the following Friday. Andrew felt powerless to help her. Kyra got the brunt of Heather's sleep deprivation as she became short-tempered about every little thing in the house. As Halloween fast approached, Heather's condition only seemed to worsen. She blanked out often and couldn't recall what she was doing half the time, often wondering how she had gotten somewhere or not knowing what she was doing or where she was.

The morning of the appointment Andrew decided it would be safer if he drove Heather to the appointment. He woke her up from the fitful sleep she was having and made her eat some cereal and have a cup of coffee.

"Where are we going today?" she asked sleepily.

"To see Dr. Kent about your problems with hearing all these things and you not sleeping," Andrew explained.

"Oh, okay," Heather said, sipping her coffee slowly.

Andrew smiled sadly at her and stroked her hair. Once she was done with her coffee and cereal, he helped her get dressed and into the car. They dropped Kyra off at school before driving into the city center to the doctors' offices. It wasn't hard to find parking since all the parking bays were free and the office park was eerily quiet. They took the elevator up to the correct floor but upon disembarking they found the floor completely abandoned. There was no sign of the nurses or of anyone being on the floor at all. Andrew sat Heather down in the waiting area and went off to see if he could find anyone in the darkened halls, but everything looked like they had left in a hurry. Most of the doors were left open and the rooms were empty with files discarded on the floor.

Disheartened, Andrew stumbled into a man dressed in a janitor uniform. "Excuse me, sir, do you know where Dr. Kent's rooms have moved to?"

"Dr. Kent, sir? The Doctor that was renting floor three?" the janitor responded.

"Yes, that's the one," Andrew said.

"Well, he up and left the other day, not a word of where he went. He didn't even pack up all his things. Just vanished he did, sir," the janitor explained.

Andrew felt a panic rising inside of him and nodded. "Right, thank you for letting me know."

Andrew went back to Heather and helped her up. "Come on, let's get you back to Dr. Jennifers and see if she can't prescribe you something to help you sleep."

"She's a general doctor," Heather mumbled. "Where's Dr. Kent?"

"It looks like he had to leave in a hurry, don't know why, but let's just get you to a doctor of some sort and get you some sleep before you fall over."

"Okay," Heather said, her eyes already drooping. Andrew got her back to the car and buckled her in, driving out of the parking bay and in the direction of their General Practitioner. He dialed the receptionist through the car to make an appointment while they were on their way.

"Dr. Jennifers' rooms, how can I help?" the bubbly blonde answered the phone as usual.

"Hi, it's Mr. Andrew Lawrence, I need an emergency appointment for my wife Heather. Is Dr. Jennifers available now?"

"An emergency appointment, sir? What is the emergency exactly?" the receptionist asked.

"It has to do with the surgery Heather had in Mexico, and I'm worried about her mental health. Please, can the doctor squeeze her in quickly? I can be there in about fifteen minutes, traffic allowing."

"Okay," the receptionist said, "I think I can squeeze you in, but you really need to be here in fifteen minutes then."

"Thank you," Andrew said, hanging up the call and putting his foot down on the gas. He wasn't going to waste the opportunity for Heather to see a doctor today.

With a few minutes to spare, Andrew pulled into the parking lot of the doctors' offices and got out the car, going around to the passenger side to open up for Heather. He took her arm and walked her into the offices.

"Hi Mr. Lawrence," the receptionist greeted him, "Dr. Jennifers is busy with a patient, but once she's done she can see you both before her next appointment. You can take a seat in the waiting room for me."

"Thank you so much," Andrew said, leading Heather to two open seats in the waiting room. It was a cheery waiting room, with a small section off to the side where children could play with toys and a small table in the center with magazines to be read. Once seated, Heather rested her head against Andrew's shoulder and dozed lightly; Andrew felt like his heart was breaking for her. She just needed a good night's sleep and she'd probably feel a thousand times better than what she was feeling.

Andrew simply sat with his own thoughts, listening to the soft snores of Heather's breathing, as they waited their turned for the doctor. All too soon the receptionist called, "Mr. and Mrs. Lawrence," and Andrew had to gently shake Heather awake, as much as he didn't want to. He helped her up and they shuffled into Dr Jennifers' room where they were greeted by their bubbly family practitioner who, upon seeing Heather, immediately became concerned about her condition and shot off a series of questions.

"It's been the last couple of days mostly that she hasn't been able to sleep. She says she hears things that keep her up at night and then she says she's started to see things; it sounds like hallucinations because when I'm with her I don't see the same things. It's scaring both of us. Then we went to see Dr. Kent but, he's taken off to God knows where," Andrew explained to Dr. Jennifers.

Dr Jennifers, a tall, thin but friendly woman with dark hair tied back, listened intently to Andrew before going to Heather who was sitting on the examination bed. "I'm just going to do a regular check-up on you, okay, Heather?"

Heather nodded and complied.

"Sleep deprivation can cause auditory and visual hallucinations; have you been under a lot of stress lately, Heather?" Dr. Jennifers asked.

"No more than usual," Heather mumbled. "Nothing I can't handle."

"Well, this could be your body's way of saying you can't handle it," Dr. Jennifers said, "I recommend taking some time off of work and just getting some rest. I'm going to prescribe a mild sleeping tablet to help you get the sleep you need, and you should find that rights most of the issues you're having."

"Thank you so much, Doctor," Andrew said, "And thank you for seeing us on such short notice."

"It's my pleasure; where I can help, I always will," Dr. Jennifers said with a small smile, sitting back down at her desk and pulling her doctor's pad towards her, scribbling the prescription down for Heather.

"I must admit the surgery amazes me. For Heather to be able to hear and speak with such clarity is simply unheard of. Dr. Kent really is working with breakthrough technology and science."

"I know, which is why we're so surprised that he just up and left like that," Andrew said, taking the prescription from her.

"Could be nothing, try reaching out and contacting him. Perhaps he had an emergency back in Mexico that he had to attend to," Dr. Jennifers said.

Andrew nodded. "That makes sense."

"Now, get this prescription filled and take Heather home, give her a nice hot bath and a cup of tea and a lot of rest. That's my best advice. Tonight she can take the medication and get a good night's rest." Dr. Jennifers stood up and handed Andrew the prescription.

"Thank you again, Doctor," Andrew said, taking the prescription and going to get Heather.

They walked out together, Heather leaning on Andrew sleepily. Andrew got her buckled into the car and drove them over to the pharmacy. He opted to let her doze in the car while he ran in to fill her prescription, and when he came out she was still dozing lightly. His heart ached in his chest for her. He climbed in and she started with fright.

"What's going on?" she asked.

"Nothing, honey," he said, "You're safe, you're okay. I'm going to take you home and run you a bath, okay?"

"Okay, love," she mumbled, leaning her head against the window.

Andrew drove them home and once there, he got her upstairs and ran her a bath. He left her to relax while he went downstairs.

Heather undressed slowly, every movement felt like a chore. She climbed into the bath and let the water soak into her body. The warm water made her feel sleepy again, and she was just about to doze off when she heard the high pitched screaming again. She sat bolt upright and looked around for the source but knew she would find none. She placed her hands over her ears to try and block it out, but nothing helped. On and on she could hear the woman shrieking in pain as though someone were gutting her with a knife. She rocked back and forth to try and comfort herself, but nothing would help and eventually it felt like she couldn't breathe.

Suddenly Andrew was pulling her out of the bath water she had sunk into and she was gasping for air.

"I've got you, I've got you," he was saying, holding her up and patting her back. "You fell asleep and sunk into the water; take deep breathes now."

Heather coughed and spluttered and spat out bath

water. There was no sound of screaming, it had all been a dream. She looked up at Andrew and burst into tears, unsure what else could possibly go wrong at this point. Andrew held her against him as much as he could and stroked her wet hair. "Come on, baby, it's okay. You're okay. I've got you."

"Why is this happening to me?" Heather blubbered out. "What did I do to deserve this?"

"You didn't do anything, baby, sometimes things just happen and we can't explain it," Andrew said, trying to sooth her.

"I want to go to church," Heather said suddenly. "I want to go to church and I want a priest to pray for me."

"Okay, baby, okay, if that's what you want to do then that's what we're going to do," Andrew said. "But for now, let's get you out of the bath and dry and into some warm clothes, okay?"

"Okay," Heather said, letting go of Andrew.

Chapter Nine

That night, after they had dinner and Kyra was settled in her room, Andrew brought Heather her medication and cup of warm milk. "Hopefully this will let you get some sleep."

Heather took the medication and used the warm milk to swallow it. She sat up and finished as much as of the warm milk as she could before the medication started to take effect. She set the glass down and snuggled into her warm bed. Andrew had climbed onto his side of the bed and snuggled against her, holding onto her.

"Sweet dreams, princess," he murmured.

"Goodnight," Heather breathed as she closed her eyes.

She didn't know how long she had been asleep for before the smell of smoke assaulted her. She struggled to rouse from her sleepy state, she put that down to the medication, but her mind screamed for her to wake. There was something horribly wrong. She could smell the smoke and feel the heat. She blinked several times, but trying to keep her eyes open was like mission impossible. They just wanted to stay closed and wanted to let her sleep some more, but every fiber in her body screamed that there was danger. She forced herself awake and slowly sat up to see her room was filled with smoke.

She coughed and spluttered and reached for Andrew but he wasn't in bed next to her. Confused, she climbed out of bed and stumbled towards the bedroom door, fighting the urge to just go back to sleep. She had to get to Kyra and she had to get her out of the house. There was a fire somewhere; they were in danger. She fell to the ground and crawled towards her daughter's room, trying to stay out of range of the smoke. When she reached Kyra's bed she found her daughter wasn't in it.

Panicked and confused, she only assumed Andrew had gotten Kyra out and was coming back for her. She had to get out of the house before it was too late. She crawled to the stairs and shakily got up, trying to still keep low. She made her way downstairs and saw the smoke bellowing from the kitchen; the front door was wide open so she tumbled out of it and onto the front lawn, coughing and spluttering. She lay there gasping for air.

"Andrew?" she called, "Kyra?"

She looked around and found the street silent and devoid of people; no one had come to assist them and her family was nowhere to be seen. She panicked once more, worried they were stuck in the house somewhere. She turned to go back in only to see the front door was shut and locked but there was no smoke. In fact there was no sign of fire at all. Confused, Heather got shakily to her feet and went to open the front door, but it was locked. Shivering in the cold, with nothing but her nightdress on, she rang the doorbell hoping it would be enough to get Andrew's attention. The landing light came on and she waited for him to open the door for her.

When door swung open, however, standing there was not her husband, but the most demonic looking thing she had ever seen. Cloven hooves and red leather skinned, with horns curling up to the sky and a great snout on its face. Heather shrieked and recoiled, bringing her hands up to cover her face.

"Heather, what are you doing out here? What's wrong?" Andrew asked.

Heather moved her hands from her face to see not a demon standing at the door, but her husband standing there in his boxer shorts.

"How did you get out here? What is going on?" Andrew asked, moving to help her up.

Heather let him help her up and followed him back inside the house. Andrew shut the door and checked her over for scrapes and bruises, but still she didn't answer him.

"Baby, how did you get outside?" Andrew asked again.

"I... There was a fire. You weren't in bed, neither was Kyra. The door was open and I was outside and then...the door was closed and I was locked outside."

"Sounds like you had another nightmare," Andrew said, rubbing her back. "I'm sorry, baby. Why don't you come back to bed now?"

"Okay," Heather said, hugging herself. "But it felt so real, Andrew."

"I'm sorry," Andrew said again, taking her arm and leading her upstairs. "I'm sure it was terrifying."

"I want to go to church tomorrow," Heather said. "Please, I really do."

Andrew nodded. "Okay, baby, we'll go to church tomorrow."

Andrew put her back in bed and tucked her in before climbing back in himself. He was started to feel the exhaustion himself. He wrapped his arms around her and held her, but he waited until she fell asleep before he felt like he could go back to sleep himself.

~

Heather forced herself to stay awake for the sermon the next morning. Kyra had wanted to take her headphones and Heather had forbade it. They had all dressed neatly and piled into the car and driven to St. Mark's Catholic Church for the Sunday morning sermon. Afterward, Heather waited back and said an extra prayer for what she was going through. Andrew ushered Kyra out of the church to give Heather her privacy. Heather had wanted to go to confession as well, but she didn't know where to start; she hadn't been to confession in years. As she made her way out of the church, she saw the priest standing in the doorway saying goodbye to his congregation and decided to seek out his advice.

"Thank you for the wonderful message, Father," she said.

"You are most welcome, my child, though we haven't seen you and your family here for some time. It was lovely to see you again and by God's gracious miracle to hear you speak and know you can hear his word."

"Thank you, Father," Heather said shyly. "I wonder if I can ask your advice on a matter."

"Speak freely, my child, you're the last one I had to see off."

"Father, I'm going through something and it's been a plague on myself and my family. I'm hearing and seeing things, demonic things, and it's ever since I've had the surgery that has enabled me to hear and speak. It's as though I've been cursed. I don't know what to do or who to turn to anymore," Heather said.

"Turn to God when all is lost, my child," the priest said, opening his hands to gesture to the heavens. "Have you sought medical assistance?"

"I have and no one has been able to assist me, Father, which is why I came here today. Last night I swore I saw the devil himself in my home. I'm scared for my soul and for the souls of my family. I don't know why this is happening to us."

The priest looked at Heather skeptically and then said, "Perhaps you should seek out the council of Father Brian from the Parish next to ours. He's more versed in this sort of thing than I am."

"He is?" Heather asked. "Do you think he could help us?"

"I will pray for you, my child, so that you find the answers you seek," the priest said. "You'll find his church on Google Maps, just search for St. Thomas Church and you'll find it. Tell him I sent you."

"Yes, thank you, Father," Heather said, before hurrying outside.

Kyra and Andrew were milling about with various church folk having tea and cake when Heather found them and quickly whispered, "We need to go to St. Thomas now."

"Why?" Andrew asked.

"Because Father Jeffrey says there's a Father Brian there who might be able to help me," Heather explained.

"Help you with what, babe?" Andrew asked, setting his teacup down on the table.

"With what's happening to me, Andrew," Heather said irritably. "Whatever is happening to me isn't natural, it's not of this world. We need to go."

"Heather, you're acting paranoid. You're sleep deprived and..."

"Stop blaming sleep deprivation," Heather said, loud enough that several people around them stopped their conversations to glance at them. "I know what I saw and the devil is coming for us, Andrew."

Andrew held his hands up. "Calm down, Heather, okay, you want to go see this priest, we'll go see this priest, but calm down."

Heather hugged herself and glanced at Kyra who was staring at her with wide eyes. Heather reached out to hug her, but Kyra shifted away from her mother which just broke her heart even more.

"I don't want to go to another church," Kyra said. "Can I stay home?"

"Sure, I'll drop you along the way," Andrew said. "Come on, let's get going."

After dropping Kyra off at the house, Andrew punched the name of the church into the GPS and started to drive towards there.

"You think I'm crazy," Heather said, after they had been driving in silence for a few minutes.

"I don't think you're crazy, I think you're really tired and I think that something is wrong that needs to be medically corrected," Andrew said.

"I know what I've seen, Andrew, and I know what I've heard," Heather said. "And you can say it's because I haven't slept and you can say it's from the surgery or from stress or from whatever, but something is wrong with me and it's more than just a medical something."

"Since when do you believe in ghosts and goblins and demons?" Andrew asked.

"Don't patronize me," Heather said. "I know what I sound like, so there's no need to make it sound worse."

"I'm not patronizing you, Heather, I just think you're really on edge and you need to be reminded of where this is all coming from. You're a sound, rational person normally. I say we go home and try see where Dr. Kent went and see if we can't get this all straightened out," Andrew said. "Besides, if I was patronizing you, would I be driving you to St. Thomas right now?"

Heather let the tears flow freely; she knew she sounded like a nut job, but she knew she was on to something. Something was wrong, and something was after her soul. She could just tell and if this Father Brian could offer her some answers, then maybe this was the way to go.

They didn't say much else for the remainder of the trip. Andrew wanted to say more but didn't want to set Heather off any more than he already had. He needed to find out where Dr. Kent was and how to reach him so he could straighten out what was happening to Heather. Maybe she just needed to see a shrink, maybe being able to hear was just messing with her head. He didn't know, he was no doctor. He just wanted to get Heather the help she needed.

For now, though, he was happy to just appease her, so he pulled into the parking lot of St. Thomas, shut the engine off, and looked at her. "Do you want me to wait here?"

"No, I want you to come with me; I'm afraid," Heather said.

"Okay, baby, I'll come with," Andrew said, unbuckling his safety belt and climbing out of his side of the car. They met in front of the car and linked hands, walking up to the church together. Opening the door, they walked into the silent chapel and looked around. There was no one in sight and for a moment, Andrew was relieved and thought they could at least tick that off the list and head home when a voice called out, "I'll be with you in a minute, my children."

It was an old but sturdy sounding voice that came from the very front of the church. Heather glanced at Andrew before leading him forward down the center aisle between the pews. Coming around the front, an elderly looking priest came down to meet them. "Hello there, how can I help you?"

"We're looking for Father Brian," Heather said meekly.

"Well, you've found him, my child, and what can I do for you?" Father Brian said.

"We were told you could help me with a problem I've been having. See, I recently had a surgery to help me hear and speak again which was a success but since then I've been hearing things that aren't there and I've also been seeing things...demonic things..."

If Father Brian was surprised he didn't let on, instead he indicated that Heather should come and have a seat in the front pew next to him. "And tell me, my child, have you been to see the doctors about this?"

"Yes, they all say it's sleep deprivation and a host of all other things, but I know what I've seen, Father, and I'm telling you I've seen the devil himself. Can you help me?" Heather said, trying her best not to let the panic take over her.

Father Brian sat quietly for a moment and then said, "I'll need the details of the doctor who did your surgery and all the information that you have. I'm not saying that anything will come of it, my child, it could honestly still be a medical issue, but I am willing to put your mind at peace and look into this for you."

"Of course, Father, thank you. Should we bring the files to you?" Heather asked. "We can come back today."

Father Brian chuckled. "That's fine, but you can email all the information to me. I'm not as out of touch with the world as some priests are. I'll give you my business card, and you can send me the information and I will look into it. I wouldn't worry about it though, my child, ninety-nine point nine percent of the time nothing comes of such things and normally it is a medical issue. Sometimes our minds have a way of running off with us."

Heather hugged herself. "I just...I feel as though something evil is haunting me and my family, Father."

"The mind is a powerful thing, my child. Now, you come fill in your details and get my business card, and I'll make sure to get back to you this week before Halloween," Father Brian said standing up. He led them to his office in the back where he produced a simple form for them to complete. Andrew was actually at ease with this, thankful that the Father was such a sensible priest and that he wasn't some old coot that was spewing mumbo jumbo about demons and heaven and hell. It was all very logical and made complete sense to Andrew and maybe this would set Heather at ease as well.

Once they were done, Andrew walked Heather back to the car and they started the drive home. Andrew could sense Heather wasn't convinced, but they at least had taken a step in the right direction.

Chapter Ten

Things did not get easier as they waited for Father Brian to get back to them. In fact, if anything, Heather's hallucinations seemed to intensify the closer they got to Halloween, and Kyra was now fearful of being around her mother. Andrew would sometimes wake in the middle of the night to find Heather rocking back and forth in bed, speaking words in another language that he did not understand. It would take him almost an hour or two to coax her back to sleep. Nothing seemed to help and no amount of begging and pleading would convince Heather that she needed to go to the hospital.

Andrew had tried to contact the facility where Dr. Kent had performed the operation, but that too had been mysteriously closed and there was no way to reach the doctor. At a loss for what to do for his wife, Andrew hoped that Father Brian would be able to reach her with reason and logic and that he would do it soon, because it seemed every day that Heather was closer to going over the edge.

The morning of Halloween Andrew woke up groggily to the smell of pancakes and bacon wafting up from the kitchen, and he wondered if he was now hallucinating himself. He got up and blearily got dressed. He found Kyra walking out of her room, roused from her own bed with the promise of tasty goodness.

"Who's cooking?" she asked.

"Must be Mom," Andrew said hesitantly.

They walked downstairs together to find that Heather was indeed making quite a spread for them. The table was set with fresh fruit cut up and freshly squeezed orange juice. There were pancakes on the table already ready to be eaten, with more on the way. Heather brought a platter of bacon to the table and with a jolly smile said, "Good morning, family, I hope you're hungry."

"Who are you and what have you done with my wife?" Andrew asked, skeptical of what he was seeing.

"What do you mean?" Heather asked, stealing a piece of bacon to nibble on as she stood at the table.

"You've been a nervous wreck for weeks and today you're making pancakes and bacon, what gives?" Andrew asked.

"I had a good night's rest is all," Heather said. "It's like you said, I just needed some sleep."

Andrew was hesitant to feel relieved, but he did feel it and smiled at Kyra. "Well, in that case, happy Halloween to the Lawrence family."

They sat down and started to eat, everyone in a jolly mood as they consumed the food Heather had prepared. Andrew would never admit it, but he ate far more than he should have and it made him feel sleepy despite only having just woken up. He gave a great yawn and smiled at Heather. "Food was great, honey. Man, I'm full."

"Why don't you go lay down for a bit?" Heather suggested. "You look exhausted."

Andrew yawned again. "No, I just got up. I have to get to work..." Andrew could feel his eyes closing against his will. He rested his arm on the table and his head against his arm and closed his eyes, falling asleep almost instantly.

"Mr. Lawrence, wake up."

"Wake up, Mr. Lawrence."

Andrew could feel someone shaking him, but it was hard fighting the sleepy feeling that had its grip over him. It was as though he was fighting against his way through a dreamy fog. He felt as though something was immensely wrong, but he couldn't pinpoint what it was. He just wanted to rest.

"Mr. Lawrence, wake up."

Again, that irritating voice commanding him to open his eyes and then the sharp smell of ammonia that brought him sharply to his senses. He opened his eyes and sat up straight, looking around the dining room of his house. He couldn't comprehend what he was seeing. The table was still set for breakfast, though there were flies buzzing around the food now. It must be late afternoon, and surrounding him were three nuns and kneeling next to him was Father Brian.

"Thank God, where are your wife and child?" Father Brian asked. "Mr. Lawrence, where are your wife and child?"

"I...I don't know. We were having breakfast..."

"Drugged," Father Brian said, "You've been drugged, no doubt by the hell bringer himself."

"Hell bringer?" Andrew asked. "What are you on about?"

"You need to get up; we need to find your wife and child and stop them before it's too late," Father Brian said, taking Andrew's arm and helping him to his feet.

"Too late for what? How did you get into my house?" Andrew looked around and a sense of panic fell onto him. "Heather?" he called. "Kyra?" he called soon after. He stumbled towards the stairs and up them, going to check the bedrooms, but found the house to be empty. "Where's my phone?"

A nun stepped forward and held out a phone to him and he dialed Heather's number, but the phone rang from the dining room table which meant she left it behind.

"They are headed to a cemetery and I'm almost certain I know which one; we must stop them from the summoning. Are you strong enough yet? We cannot waste any more time," Father Brian said with urgency in his voice.

"What summoning? What are you talking about?" Andrew said, grabbing the priest by the shoulders. "Where are they?"

"I will explain everything in the car; come with us now, Mr. Lawrence. We need to save your family before they can complete the ritual," Father Brian said, leading them out to a minibus parked in front of the house. Andrew followed, not sure what he was doing.

"Why don't we call the police?" Andrew asked. "Surely, they can help."

"They won't believe us and even if they do, they'll simply arrest your wife and that won't solve the problem. We must release her from the hell bringer's possession."

"You think Heather is possessed?" Andrew asked.

"She is," Father Brian said as he started the minibus, "by someone named Colin Kent, brother to your dear Dr. Kent, and a Satanist who was gunned down by police while trying to summon the devil and sacrifice a virgin child."

"Wait, what? How do you know this?" Andrew asked.

"I found out while digging up information on Dr. Kent. It turns out Dr. Kent is also a Satanist who transplanted pieces of his brother into your wife and used a Satanic ritual to transfer his soul as well. It isn't hallucinations your wife is having; she is seeing and hearing Colin."

"You expect me to believe this?" Andrew said. "Stop the car and let me out."

"I can do that," Father Brian said, "but your wife is possessed, and she is going to sacrifice your child to Satan this Hallows Eve in a bid to summon him to the mortal plane if we don't stop him and evict that soul from your wife's body. Is that a chance you're willing to take? Speak now."

Andrew fell silent, conflicted over what to believe, but he didn't ask to get out again. He simply let Father Brian drive, and they fell into an uneasy silence. The sun began to set and Father Brian pushed the minibus to go faster, muttering to himself about time and when they would perform the ritual. Andrew felt all kinds of anxiety as they drove and wondered if this wasn't some sort of prank that Heather was playing on him. If he didn't know her better he would say it was, but Heather wasn't the pranking type.

Father Brian finally spoke up, "We're nearly there. It's imperative that we get your daughter away from your wife. You must distract your wife while the nuns secure your daughter. She will be safe with them."

Andrew simply nodded. "How many people do you think will be there?"

"Dr. Kent might be there along with your wife; I'm not sure if any of their followers will be there, hopefully not," Father Brian said. "We will have to pray not."

Andrew swallowed hard and the palms of his hands itched with sweat. He felt like a mad man driving into a cemetery with the priest and the nuns. They parked and climbed out of the minibus before Father Brian led them further in amongst the gravestones. "This way," he whispered as he walked, leading them. It was creepy to be in the cemetery on Halloween night, but what was even creepier was after walking for some time, Andrew saw some candles lit ahead and heard some weird chanting coming from the distance.

"That's her," Father Brian said, "and from the sounds of it, it's just two of them."

"Let's go get them," Andrew said.

"We need to be careful; we don't know if Satan has given this soul any demonic powers," Father Brian said. "I will do my best to exorcise her quickly." He added the last part, taking out his bible and crossing himself. Andrew also crossed himself before they walked forward once again, the nuns going around the side.

Andrew couldn't believe his eyes as they approached the grave where Heather and Dr. Kent were kneeling. Kyra was bound on top of a large grave and was clearly crying in fear from what Andrew could see. Heather and Dr. Kent were kneeling in front of her, chanting in a strange language that sounded like Latin.

"Heather," Andrew called, "Heather, what are you doing?"

Dr. Kent and Heather both stopped chanting and turned to look at them.

"I'll deal with this," Dr. Kent said and got up. "You continue the ritual." He grabbed a shovel and came towards Andrew and Father Brian aggressively as Heather started to chant again.

"What are you doing, Dr. Kent?" Andrew said, holding his hands up.

Dr. Kent didn't answer and instead took a swing at both of them. They both backed away as he swung again. Andrew looked around for anything he could use as a weapon, but he couldn't see anything in the vicinity. The third swing came dangerously close to connecting with him so he backed up some more.

"Please let my wife and daughter go; they haven't done anything to you," Andrew begged.

"In the name of Christ," Father Brian began to yell, and Dr. Kent turned to face him. Andrew took this as an opportunity and lunged at him, tackling him to the ground and wrestling him for the shovel that he held. Father Brian ran towards Heather while Andrew fought with Dr. Kent. Fists started to fly and Andrew gave as good as he got, although Dr. Kent seemed to be in better shape than Andrew was. Andrew didn't let up though and soon he had the high ground and was on top of Dr. Kent, and he rained down punches as hard and as fast as he could muster them, his fists throbbing in pain as he did so. There was a commotion coming from where Heather was, but Andrew didn't let it distract him. He managed to hit Dr. Kent hard enough to stun him, so Andrew had time to scramble up and get the shovel which he swing and hit Dr. Kent in the head with. He wasn't sure if the man was dead or just out cold, but he didn't stick around to see. He ran for where he had last seen his wife.

Two nuns passed him with Kyra as he ran towards the grave site, and he was grateful she was at least safe. When he got there he was horrified to see that two other nuns were holding Heather down and Father Brian was standing over her chanting in

Latin himself. He wanted to approach, but at the same time he didn't want to interfere.

"Daddy," Kyra called; she had escaped the nuns and had come running back to be with Andrew. "What's going on? What are they doing to Mommy?"

"They're trying to save her," Andrew explained, hugging Kyra tightly.

Father Brian continued to chant and Andrew couldn't believe his eyes, but it seemed to him that Heather's face contorted into a disfigured face of a man. When she screamed, her voice was distorted from her own; it sounded like a thousand voices screaming at once. Father Brian was yelling his chants at this point when suddenly there was a shriek from Heather and a flash of bright light from where they were holding her down.

~

*H*eather walked into her company with Jeremy by her side and was happy to see everyone working hard. It had been a tough time since Halloween, but everything was right in the world once more. After she had woken up in the hospital and Andrew had explained everything to her, she had never been so grateful before to see her little family and to know that everything was going to be alright.

"Hi Heather, I have the reports you wanted and there's a call for you on line two," Kayla said as she walked in.

"Thank you, Kayla," Heather signed, turning the phone onto speaker so Jeremy could translate for her.

"Heather, this is Father Brian, I just wanted to check how you are doing?"

"Much better thank you, Father," Jeremy translated for her.

"I'm just so sorry you lost your hearing and voice again; it is such a pity."

"I'm not, I could have lost so much more," Heather signed as Jeremy spoke. "I'm just grateful that you believed me and you came when you did. Thank you again, Father Brian. What of Dr. Kent?"

"The police are looking for him and once they find him, they will arrest him and that will be the end of that. You have nothing to worry about. Take care, my dear."

"Thank you, Father, and see you in church on Sunday."

Father Brian hung up the call and Jeremy smiled at Heather, signing, "You're really not sad that you can't hear or speak anymore?"

Heather shrugged. "I prefer the silence to be honest. It was way too noisy for my liking."

She pulled the reports to her and started to working, without another word but with a small smile on her face.

To Watch - Coming Soon

The Demon Cat Khristmas Specials

Killer Kitteh Khristmas

Merry Meow - Coming soon

Jingle Fur - Coming soon

Stand Alones

The Culling

#RIPJohn

Belladonna

Buried

The Witches of Harbour

Hex - Coming Soon

Shh... - Coming Soon

The Priestess - Coming Soon

The Reaper- Coming Soon

FANTASY TITLES

A Spacehiker Adventure

Unlikely Hero

Hidden in Plain Sight - Coming Soon

Homeward Bound - Coming Soon

MURDER MYSTERY TITLES

Bullseye - Coming Soon

Stones - Coming Soon

PARANORMAL ROMANCE TITLES

Balancer Books

Neutral Ground - Coming Soon

Holy Demons - Coming Soon

Born in South Africa, in the heart of Johannesburg, Sian Claven grew up with a vivid imagination. When she wasn't immersing herself in books, she was actively creating her own stories.

At 29 years old, left to her own devices after her sister immigrated, Sian, wrote her first horror book Ensnared and dared to publish it under the guidance of indie authors Toni Cox and Ashleigh Giannaccaro.

Now she has released more than ten books including a thriller and sci-fi fantasy.

In 2019, Sian took up the challenge of publishing 11 books in 11 months.

Sian came second place in the First Annual Indie Awards for Favourite African Author.

Sian's book, Sylvana, the final book in her Butcher series, made the Amazon top 100 best sellers list in several categories across three countries.

In 2020 Sian reached International Best Seller status with her story Shh... as part of the Soul's Day box set and her story Neutral Ground with the Possessed by Passion box set.

In her spare time, Sian is an avid Harry Potter fan, pop collector and Bingo addict. She resides in Johannesburg with her 2 best friends, their 6 dogs and 2 cats.

You can follow her using her handle @sianbclaven
on:
Facebook
Twitter
Instagram
Goodreads
Visit her website now:
www.sianbclaven.com

www.ingramcontent.com/pod-product-compliance
Lightning Source LLC
Chambersburg PA
CBHW021400150726
47989CB00005B/2326